Copyright 2011, JT Kalnay

This is a work of fiction. While, as in all fiction, the story is based on experiences, real or imagined, all names, characters, places, and incidents are either products of my overactive imagination or are used fictitiously. No reference to any real person is intended or should be inferred.

Discover other titles by jt Kalnay at:
www.jtkalnay.com

This book is available in print at most online retailers.

License Notes

This book is licensed for your personal enjoyment only. This book may not be re-sold or given away to other people. If you would like to share this book with another person, please purchase an additional copy for each recipient. If you're reading this book and did not purchase it, or it was not purchased for your use only, then please purchase your own copy.

Be Sure to Read All JT Kalnay's Novels

From Smashwords #1 Best Selling Author

The Pattern

jt kalnay

From Smashwords #1 Best Selling Author

Obsession for Vengeance

jt kalnay

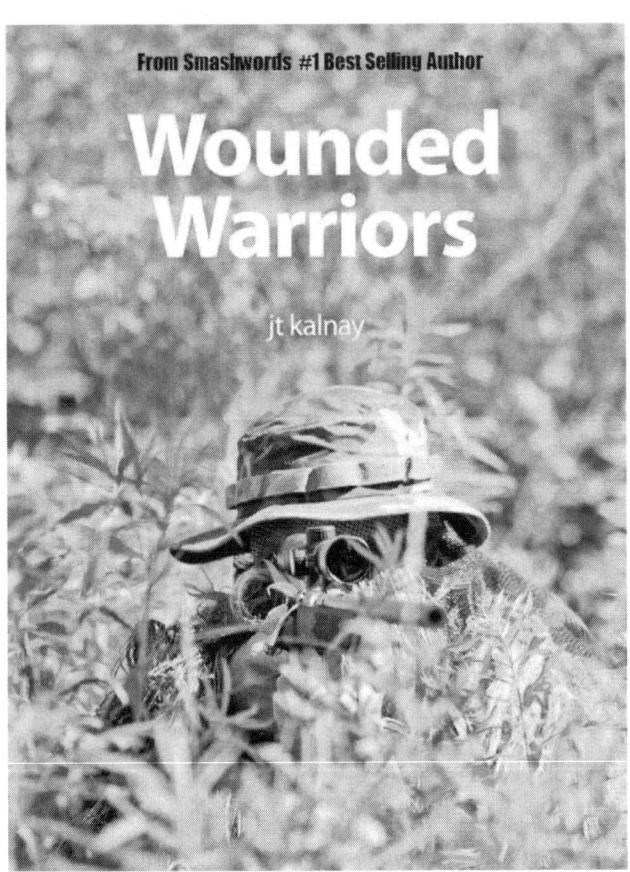

Mina's Eyes
jt Kalnay

Dorgali

Martina looked back over her shoulder to savor the valley, the clay tiled roofs in the Sardinian town, and the mountains beyond. Its beauty washed over her, and for one moment she was at peace. Tranquility. Where had it gone? Had it vanished forever on that windswept beach? Or did it simply lay dormant, waiting, for a time like this, for a place like this, and for a man she could love. If she could ever love again.

Martina turned back to the rock, chalked her strong hands, and started up. Her blue gray Nordic eyes explored, discovered, then caressed pockets, edges, and other imperfections in the near perfect limestone. Her hands and feet glided ever upwards in a vertical dance, reminiscent of her days on the stage, filled with grace and power. Sometimes the movements took her back to when her long lost daughters had danced alongside her in their gossamer gowns as Tchaikovsky soared and filled the theater and set souls free. But today the rhythm took her elsewhere, nowhere near those memories, but rather up and up, over the roofs, over the valley, over the limestone cliff to the heights above.

Kane watched her as she ascended. His back against an ancient pine that had been twisted by the wind, his pack lay at his feet. He'd seen her here before, a few days ago, and had returned each day hoping to see her again, thinking this time the spell would be broken, his words would be freed, and he could speak again. Kane climbed too. But not like Martina. He understood her mastery, knew on some level that only a few could do what she did, and maybe none better. That first day, after she'd gone, he'd tried the routes she'd climbed. Impossible to him. Couldn't make the first moves. And she'd climbed them alone, no partner, no rope, no bonds.

At his hotel he'd Googled her, because he thought he'd recognized her. Not as a climber, but as a dancer. A dancer he thought he'd met, or at least seen before. He was almost certain he'd found her, learned who she was. Her face was unique. High Russian cheekbones draped with deep Argentinean skin. But it was those graceful ballet like steps that gave the most important clue, even though her right leg moved differently than her left. Article after article on page after page detailed her long career, her ascension to the Bolshoi, her mastery of the art, her romances with Baryshnikov, and others. Her crippling injury and forced retirement. And then the story ended almost completely just three years earlier. More searching, hours unending, and Kane finally found an article, an obituary, in a Buenos Aries newspaper, and then Kane understood why the pages ended, why she had withdrawn from the spotlight, from the worldwide forum that she had ruled, both on and off the stage.

"La Regina" the articles had called her. But no more. In his emergency room, "the emerge", his refuge, he'd witnessed firsthand the carnage wrought on those left behind, and he had used it remorselessly in his writing, without conscience. The second story, or was it the first, or tenth? They had made him rich, and for a while, not so much famous as notorious. But no more. There had been no words in many years.

He watched her finish the climb, then he stood and walked towards her at a pace he hoped would put him at the base of the cliff at the precise moment that she would arrive back in the horizontal domain. His heart beat faster, his mouth went dry, and he realized he had no idea what to say, or how to say it. He was, quite simply, at a loss for words. He recognized that this was both an ironic and, lately, chronic state.

At the base of the cliff, Martina sat in the early morning sun. Her long blonde hair whisped over her bronzed shoulder by the gentle Mediterranean breeze. She drank and smiled, half closed her eyes. In repose, the little damages melted away, and she was at peace, at rest.

"Bon giorno," Kane said.

She lifted her chin, opened only one eye, and answered softly, "Bon giorno".

Kane pointed at the cliff while he pantomimed climbing.

"This piece is very hard, mas difficile."

"Si," she replied. Her chin dropped, her eye closed in partial dismissal.

"Can I ask you something? To show me something?" Kane asked.

Her chin lifted again, her eye opened again, registering partial, but only partial interest. Kane dropped his pack, removed a rope, and pointed at the climb.

"Can you show me how you did, how you did..." his voice

drifted off, perplexed, stymied by the words he did not know. So he turned a hip, extended a leg, placed his hand just so, and rocked his weight towards his hand.

She watched his dance. Drank. Thought. She looked at his deep tan, his thinning hair, his wiry frame and tight forearms. She considered his face, thought she saw something genuine, and no awe. No fawning, no grasping, no desperation for a smile or word, for a moment of her time. Just an older man, looking at a woman, a climber asking another climber for advice on how to move. She drank again.

"Si," she said, surprising herself.

"Grazi," Kane said after the lesson.

He extended his hand to shake hers. She took it. Their calloused fingers and calloused hands clasped firmly, solidly. For a moment their eyes met while their hands remained clasped. And then, surprising herself again, she stepped towards him and kissed the air beside both his cheeks.

"Prego," she answered.

Kane began coiling the rope. Martina also began packing.

"You go?" she asked. She pointed down the trail, down the valley, towards the orange tiled roofs and narrow alleys in the town.

"Si," Kane answered, "to Cala Gognone, not Dorgali."

"Me too," Martina said. "I walk."

"I hitched a ride," Kane said.

"Will you walk with me?" Martina asked.

"Sure," Kane managed.

"I think you are a good man," Martina said, "and it is too far for a good man to go alone. You come?"

Kane thought about all the days and miles and hallways he'd walked alone these last lonely years of self-imposed exile. The gaping emptiness that was his constant companion threatened for a moment to consume him, to draw him in and sink him in the morass of self-doubt and self-loathing that had been his companion these last years. Then it released him ever so slightly. He breathed deeply, more deeply than he had since, well, since before. It was like that. There was before, and there was now.

"Si," he answered.

"Thank you for the walk," Kane said.

"Prego," Martina answered.

They stood just outside her hotel, an ancient seaside home run by two Sardinian brothers, both of whom glared proprietarily out the open front door. The late morning sun dazzled off the bay by the beach. He fumbled for something to say. In their hour long walk from the cliff to the town neither had spoken. For Martina it had been one of the most pleasant hours in recent memory. Spent with a man, a good-looking older man, a man who climbed, though not so well, who could ask for her help, and who could walk through the most beautiful, most amazing countryside without intruding on her thoughts as she let it all just become part of her. For Kane it had been both heaven and hell. Ecstasy and torture. To walk alongside such a beautiful, talented, and masterful woman and to be unable to think of a single word to say.

"Where you stay?" Martina asked, realizing Kane would not speak.

"At the Hotel Cala Luna," Kane said. "They have an excellent chef. Would, would you like to have lunch with me after you get cleaned up?"

"You think I need cleaned up?" Martina asked.

"No, not really, you look great."

Her laugh interrupted his fumbling stammer.

"I sorry, I tease you, I sorry," she said.

"So. Lunch?" he asked again.

"No," Martina answered. "No lunch. For the walk, grazi."

"My pleasure," Kane said. "Prego." He hitched up his pack, smiled a sad and happy smile at her and set off up the hill to his hotel. Proud that after all this time he had fulfilled a promise and finally asked a woman out to lunch, yet very sad that she had said no, and in remembering the promise.

"Kane," she called up the hill.

He turned. She walked up the street towards him.

"You climb tomorrow? With me?" she asked.

"Si," he said.

"You hold the rope?"

"Si."

"Buono. You meet me here at seven, in the morning, okay?"

"Si," he said again.

"Arriva derci," she said, and for the second time that day she kissed the air beside his cheeks, gently placing her hand on his shoulder as she raised up on tip toes for one last kiss in the air.

Her touch, on his skin. Kane felt the touch, and felt words somewhere inside, near the source, a place that he had not visited in all these years.

Cala Luna

Early morning mist swirled around the moon-shaped bay as Kane waited across the street from Martina's rooms. Already the heat was building, and soon the sun would clear the mist from the air that would become scented with complicated mixes of the Mediterranean morning. Martina emerged just before seven, wearing her long blonde hair in a loose ponytail that she had draped forward over her shoulder and onto her black tank top. Kane stifled a gasp as she stepped across the street, put her hand on his shoulder, and kissed the air beside his ear.

That touch, again that touch. *Mina's touch*. More words fought their way through. Unbidden, unforced, simply arriving, the way it had been before, when the words and the pages had been easy. When that part of him had been free and present and a real part of him, not part of an imagined past.

"We go," she said. "Andale. We hurry."

"Where?" Kane asked.

But she was already three steps ahead, and widening the gap with every graceful stride.

"Vaya. Andale," she called over her shoulder.

Martina stopped by a small white Zodiac boat held at the bow by an olive skinned boy. A deeply tanned man fiddled with the boat controls, looking at his watch every minute.

"Tesio!" she called, and the man looked up. He stepped across the bow, onto the quay, and Martina swept him into her arms. Tesio hugged her, then stepped back, looked her up and down, and said something in Italian, recognizable as both flattering and flirtatious simply by tone. Martina laughed, what might have been a giggle in a girl, but was a seductive laugh in a woman. Kane fought and failed the urge to be jealous.

"We're going on that?" Kane asked.

"Si. Come on. We must hurry to be there in time."

Kane stepped into the rubber boat, arms extended, seeking balance on what seemed to be a flimsy, inherently unstable watercraft. He sat in the bow where Tesio pointed and soon they were speeding across the clear blue sea towards towering cliffs rising straight out of the water some miles away. Martina sat beside Tesio near the controls where they chattered loudly and incessantly. Kane heard only a few words from his perch in the foam-sprayed bow and understood only a few of those. Freed from the duty of conversation, he marveled at the white then orange brown cliffs as they raced by. One cliff loomed above the rest, and they were heading exactly in its direction. As they approached, it grew and grew, changing from cliff to mountain. Kane turned around, caught Martina's eye, and pointed to the cliff.

"Si," she said, and smiled. In that smile Kane saw happiness and freedom and adventure and none of the sadness he was convinced that Martina must still feel. Later, Kane would realize this was the exact moment that he fell completely in love. Though many say there is no moment when people fall in love, that there is no before and after in love, that there is simply a process that grows until one knows they are in love. Perhaps this is how it is for other people in other places in other times, but for Kane there would always be the moments before Martina's smile on the boat ride to Cala Luna and all the moments after. He would capture that moment in verse, and forever after when he recited the words "Cala Luna" he would channel this moment and be brought instantly back to this reality, to this moment, that divided all the before from all the after.

Martina jumped across the bow and landed between two white boulders on the powdery white sand at the base of the towering orange cliff. Tesio tossed over her pack and then launched Kane's. Kane jumped over and Martina steadied him in the sand as he wobbled once, then again.

"The boat ride was no good for you?" she asked.

"My stomach," Kane said.

"You be fine," she said. "Andale. Come on, we hurry."

"Why?" Kane said.

"You see," she answered.

She set out along the beach, her long long legs and bare feet gliding her effortlessly over the brilliant white sand while Kane ploughed deep furrows and lagged behind yet again. Ahead, the sea nipped from both sides at a moss-covered rocky path that lead out to a tiny and rapidly disappearing dry path at the base of a separate spire rising directly from the water. The spire was surrounded on all sides by sharp rocks lurking just above then just below the rising and falling waves.

"You see Kane? The water, she rises. In a few more minutes the path and the beach she is gone. We start right away. Vaya. Andale."

Kane did see. Both the low tide and the high tide marks. The salt and the seaweed.

"This is going to be an adventure," Kane said.

"Si. Adventure. Like Indiana Jones. We climb."

"My hands are wet," Kane said.

"Use some of my chalk," Martina said.

"Chalk?"

"For your hands. Like a gymnast."

Martina dipped her hands in a small bag hanging off the back of her climbing harness. She rubbed them together, then blew off the excess.

"Like that," Martina said.

Kane tentatively dipped first one hand, then the other, into her chalk bag. He rubbed them together, but there was no excess.

"You need more than that," Martina said. "Get more."

Kane put his right hand into her chalk bag and dug around, accidentally brushing the bag against her bottom.

"Sorry," he said.

Martina looked back over her shoulder, smiled a coy smile, and winked.

"Is okay, by accident," she said.

Kane put his left hand in, dug around, and not so accidentally brushed the bag against her again.

"Sorry," he said.

"Once is accident Kane, twice is something else," Martina said.

"Sorry," Kane repeated.

The ocean reached out behind them, the beach and cliffs in front. The late morning sun dazzled in the clear Mediterranean sky. Martina dangled her legs off the top of the spire as she savored her tenth olive of the morning. Kane chewed a prosciutto and mozzarella sandwich more flavorful than any he could have imagined, thankful that Martina had packed a lunch for both of them, if her ten olives could be called "lunch".

Together they looked across the dozens of yards to the sandy beach where hundreds swam and tanned and played in the surf. The blue sea dissolved into the foam of the surf and reached up onto the brilliant sand. Peace, by the shore, in her company. Peace, like he had known, but not for so long.

More than a few had gawked and pointed as Martina and Kane had climbed the needle of rock in the early morning sun. The gawkers had since returned to their tans and wine and sand castles and dozes in the mid-day heat.

"In a few hours, the water she goes down again, and then we go back," Martina said. "But now, manga, siesta."

Martina stood, removed all her clothes, dropped them near her pack, and stretched out on the rain and wind smoothed limestone summit. Kane's throat went dry. He tried not to look, tried not to look a second time, and then surrendered. Stared. The gasp he had stifled in the morning could not be stifled this time. She was glorious. Tanned, fit, proportioned, and aglow with the success of the morning's climb. Though he had seen his wife naked many times, and though he regularly saw women naked in his emergency room, she was like nothing he had ever imagined, let alone witnessed. He blinked, swallowed, and felt a heat where there had been none for years.

"Is okay Kane. In Argentina we are naked in the sun. It is not a disgraceful thing like in Canada."

Kane smiled, took off his shirt and socks and shoes, but retained his shorts. He stretched out beside her and smiled the contented smile known only to a man lying next to a naked Nordic/Argentinean beauty sun-bathing in the Mediterranean sun. After a while, just as he started to doze, he felt her hand touch his. Was he awake? Was this a dream? Her voice came to him, just barely audible over the whispering of the waves on the beach and against the spire.

"Are you a good man Kane?" she asked.

"I try. But a man can never always be a good man."

"I think you try too much," she said. She patted his hand, then rolled onto her back. Kane's second gasp was greater than the first.

At the low tide they picked their way across the still wet and slippery rocks until they reached the beach. As soon as they reached the burning white sand, first one, then another and another approached her until a small group had gathered around Martina. The bolder ones posed questions, the less bold simply stared and smiled. Cameras were pointed, autographs were sought. Kane quietly stepped just beyond the edge of the group. Out of the sun, into a shadow. He felt the sunburn under his clothes.

He'd known such crowds, even reveled in them for a brief while. But then he had resisted them, hid from them, and now, today, he sought to slip away quietly. Martina caught his eye and nodded, *is okay, is just for a minute*.

At the edge of the crowd, an obviously American man asked Kane, "Who is she?"

"A former ballerina. The best. Quite famous actually."

The American looked at Kane.

"So what's a ballet dancer doing mountain climbing?" the American asked.

Kane shrugged.

"And you swam out there and climbed that thing with her?"

"We got here early, went across at low tide."

Kane waited for the next question. But now he saw the workings of the mind on the face of the American. Felt the mental task being undertaken by the American. The struggle to put a face to a name, a name to a face, a memory to the name and face.

"Aren't you?"

"Yes," Kane cut him short. Unable to lie, to say no, to maybe avoid the inevitable just once. How easy it would be to lie, to avoid the interaction. But he couldn't, or wouldn't, and thus the oft-repeated sequence began again.

"I love your work," the American said.

"Thanks."

And then Kane saw 'the look'. The one that meant the American had just remembered. Remembered it all. Had felt the tumblers slide into place and the memory come clear after the struggle and then realize the awkward thing, realize not just who Kane was, but what Kane was, and what had happened. It froze them. All of them. Without exception. To where at least momentarily they couldn't think of what to say next. Kane hitched up his pack and signaled to Martina that he was going to walk down the beach. It was always the same. Even here. After all these years. Always. Recognition, then a cliché, something inane, and then 'the look'. He hated the look. Despised the look. Loathed it, feared it, did everything he could to avoid it. Wished he'd never see it again. Had locked himself as far away from the world as he could for many years, speaking only to patients and friends. While he walked away from the American, and away from Martina, he tried and then understood to be impossible the hurt he would feel if the look ever appeared on Martina's beautiful beautiful face.

He sat against a wave worn boulder, looking out to sea, hiding in the shade, feeling the sunburn began to hurt. Just a little while had turned into an hour. Martina approached, stood to the side.

"May I?" she asked, pointing the sand beside him.

"Si," he answered.

She sat beside him. He felt her shoulder against his arm, her hip against his.

"I'm sorry that took so long."

"It's okay," Kane answered.

"Still I sorry. So I tell you. Once upon a time, that's how a fairy tale begins, no? Once upon a time I used to be a dancer," she said.

"I know," he answered.

"You know?" Her words were shorter, clipped, suspicious.

"Yes."

"Is that why you want to be with me? To climb with me? Because I was a dancer?" The words were an accusation.

"No."

"Por que?"

He sensed that she had been here before, and that nothing but the truth, the whole truth, the naked unvarnished truth would suffice. He breathed deeply, let it out, let duplicity and excuses and defense leave him with the cleansing breath, and began.

"At first, when I first saw you climb, I wanted to be with you because the way you moved somehow liberated me. It made me feel like anything was possible. And today, just because you are you, and *you* asked *me*, after our climb and our walk yesterday. I know you are Martina Fucentese. I even saw you once at the

Bolshoi, it was twenty seven years ago. Quite a coincidence. I have a program that you signed. You were just a girl. You touched my hand." His mind drifted back all those years, to that dance, to that touch.

"Anyway. That was then, when you were Martina Fucentese. I didn't recognize you at first. But now I do, and now we are here. And you are just Martina. Not Martina Fucentese, ballerina. Just Martina, at least to me. Mina. Can you be just Mina to me?"

Martina took his hand, smiled a grateful, humble smile. A warm smile. The accusation dissipated, then disappeared, borne away on the Mediterranean breeze.

"You have a way with words," she said. Her tone was mischievous. Was it hinting at a meaning?

"Occasionally I say something right," Kane answered slowly, feeling his way.

"I know too Kane. I know who you are."

"You know?"

"Yes. I find out. Yesterday, the manager of my rooms he told me that the manager of your rooms told him that he has a famous writer staying with him. So in the afternoon I go to the library and look in the pages and see your face on the pages on the computer. But not so much now. Just before."

Kane looked out at the ocean. But for the curvature of the earth his stare might have reached across to the other side.

"Then you don't know it all."

"Is there more to know?"

"I'll tell you. And if you don't want to be with me anymore then I'll understand. Because no-one who has ever heard this story has ever been the same. It changes them, or, more correctly, it changes who I am in their eyes. Always for the worse, usually fatally."

"Tell me," she said.

"Yes. I suppose it is good to tell, right at the start. Before too much happens."

"Begin," she said.

Again he inhaled deeply, controlled the outflow, released fear in the exhalation. Used the cleansing breath to buy a moment to collect his thoughts, to consider where to begin. He decided to begin at the beginning, and to go to the end, and to not miss any points in between.

She held his hand while the tale stretched out and on and through. She held it tighter as he reached the end. As the final words were washed out to sea in the foam of the breaking waves she turned towards him, looked directly in his eyes, and kissed both his cheeks, not the air beside.

Mina's kiss, by the sea. More words pushed their way into his mind and he felt the old itch, felt the twitch in his fingers as they sought the phantom pen. Mina's kiss.

Mist

A dense low mist clung to the pre-dawn harbor and its seaside town of Cala Luna. Kane's heart beat hard with the effort of his before breakfast run. Though it was hard to see through the fog of the bay and the fog of the effort to run over the long steep hills, Kane could clearly see back through the last several days with Martina. Could see her movements, her smile, wisps of her long blonde hair blowing in a cliffside breeze. Could hear her words, and in turn could hear his own. Not just those he'd spoken, but others that had formed somewhere else, others that might be something, a poem perhaps, or an opening, a beginning. He could see that she had already changed him, and would continue to change him. That she was someone after whom he would never be the same. He had not decided whether that was a good thing, but he had decided he wanted, needed to find out. Wanted, needed to know more.

Years had gone by since he'd had that feeling. All the years since the ultimate conclusion of his wife's inevitable decline, and even a few before. Where had they gone? His words? Had they been stolen, or had he put them away so cruelly, so forcefully, and so often that they had simply decided to stay away? And how had this happened? It had to be Mina.

He'd never believed his contemporaries who spoke about their muses. Always thought of them as weak in relying on someone else for something that could only be found within. Pooh-poohed their exuberance and adolescent crushes. But now he wondered if maybe there was something to it, if maybe they had felt something he had not felt. If maybe even something so individual and personal and selfish as writing could be more than a solitary activity. If maybe the channeling he'd felt at times with pen in hand was in fact that, an intimate connection to others through observation and reportage. He shivered with the coolness of the fog, the fear of the revelation, the loss of independence.

Kane slowed to a trot, and then to a walk. The morning mist still hung thick in spots, especially here at the water's edge. His footsteps crunched in the seaside rocks and echoed off the nearby cliffs. Tiny waves lapped at the weeds and pushed up at the tide line. The margin. Where water met rock, where sea met land. "Mina's eyes, where sea meets land." More words, coming faster now, coming in the old way, the way he remembered.

Kane stopped and bent forward, stretching his hamstrings. Beads of sweat dripped and dropped onto the polished rocks in which he stood. He heard quiet footsteps in the fog. First in front, and then to the side, echoing back off the cliff through the mist. The sound in front grew closer.

He could barely make her out, but he knew it had to be her. *Serendipitous*, he thought. An unplanned quiet moment on a silent shore with his muse approaching. She was walking slowly along the margin, looking into the water, stopping to pick up and then discard small rocks, shells. He waited, stretched, and waited some more, until he was afraid he would startle her if he waited much longer. Slowly he scuffled a foot in the rocks. Equally slowly she brought her eyes towards him.

"I see you first," she said without looking up, returning to her unhurried pace of steps, stops, and picks. "From back there."

Kane smiled, knew she was right, and stretched a little more, until she was right beside him.

"Bella serra," he said.

"Bon giorno," she answered. She kissed the air beside his cheeks. "You are wet," she said.

"I was running."

"Si. I wondered if I would see you," she said.

"You did?" he answered eagerly.

"Si," she answered.

Kane saw her amused yet comforting smile.

"You are very tired?" she asked. "From your run? From our days of climbing?"

"Un poco."

"Too tired to paddle with me later?" she asked.

"Paddle?"

"Si. Paddle. Is the right word no? Paddle. The kayak."

"It's the right word."

"So. Too tired to paddle?"

"No. Not after a shower and a good breakfast."

"Buono. Meet me there, by the pier, at ten. We paddle. A long paddle."

Martina stepped slowly away, continuing in her earlier

direction, continuing along the margin. Had she taken a step over? A step back? She stopped, picked up a small shell, regarded it, kept it, and stepped slowly farther down the shore. Kane watched her until she disappeared into the mist.

By ten o'clock the mist was gone and the blue sky reached off to infinity. When he looked up his scientist mind saw the atmosphere, but his writer's mind saw the forever of it. Felt the on and on and on of the perpetual, welcoming, impenetrable blue above, and married it to the infinite blue of her eyes. He wrinkled his nose at the cliché, but left it alone, as a memory on which he could call, a memory on which he could rely. The seaside cliffs stretched down the shore in the brilliant Mediterranean sun, disappearing where sky and water and rock merged. His people believed that spirits lived where elements met, at waterfalls, and beaches, and cliffs. At the margins. Surely in a place like this the spirits must be enchanted. Mina's eyes, where sea meets sky, where rock meets water. More words.

The clear blue ocean was warm and calm. Kane sat in the back of the long, sit-on-top ocean kayak. Schools of small fish loitered amongst the waving dancing sea grass that grew between the enormous boulders on the ocean floor where a solitary predator circled just outside the intimate zone of danger. Kane and Martina paddled slowly in time, a steady, relaxed, yet powerful rhythm into which they had settled without words or plan or thought. His mind thought about the trite poetry he had written in college, lovers' hearts beating in time and all that. So many words forgotten for so long. It's how he'd started. With the poems. The poems he'd begun to think about again. He thought that maybe a poem would be the way back. He liked the writing, missed it, craved the outlet, the release, the purity of the confession. So maybe a poem was the way, and Mina the guide.

They paddled parallel to the shore, close in to the cliffs. It was still so calm they had no fear of being dashed onto the rocks by a large wave, or of Kane's upset stomach coming back like on the Zodiac speedboat ride. They paddled in silence. A comfortable quiet this time for Kane. He no longer worried about having something brilliant or witty to say to Martina, who he now thought of as just "Mina". So quickly she had become "Mina", no longer Martina, no longer the retired world-famous dancer, or apparently equally as talented rock climber, just his new acquaintance, who might one day, in other circumstances, in other places, with more time, be a friend, or more. He knew she enjoyed their being together, but also knew she savored the quiet, his quiet. Especially in such a beautiful setting and with someone who so clearly worshipped her. Worship. Such a strong word, and yet so appropriate, and after just these few days. Though the worship itself could not be more inappropriate. Irony, to have the perfect word for the most imperfect emotion.

He thought about her here on the water. Thought that she was as comfortable in this place here on the water as she was on the rock. Thought "she is Mina of the rock and of the water." Thought "Mina's eyes, where waves meet sky..." Thought maybe there was something there. "That's good," he thought, or maybe even spoke quietly. He repeated it once, twice, three times. His memory trick when no pen was at hand.

"Okay, paddle us slow," she said.

She laid her paddle in the kayak between them, removed a pair of binoculars from her waterproof bag and scanned the cliffs. Up, down, left, further left.

"In there," she pointed to the left, towards an opening in the cliff.

"The cave?" Kane asked.

"Si," she answered.

She placed the binoculars back in her bag, and removed a large, six battery flashlight. She clicked it on, then off, then turned to Kane.

"Very slowly okay?"

"Yes dear," he answered.

Martina rolled her eyes, smiled, and turned back to the entrance of the cave.

"Along this side for a few meters," she said. "Just until is too dark."

Kane paddled the kayak very slowly, holding it steady against the small waves and the tide. He thought how lucky he was for the calm, thought that entering this cave in the big waves of their first time on the sea would be suicide. He made a mental note to constantly monitor the waves, to be alert for the slightest increase in the sea state, lessons learned from all his years spent near the water.

"A few more meters," she said. "I am looking."

"Yes," he answered.

"For a new route to climb."

"Si," he answered.

She worked slowly, shining the light up and down, back and forth in the cave.

"Something hard, but where no-one can watch, and where I can work even if it rains. There is a rainy season here."

There was so much to parse in that one sentence. Kane understood that sometimes she wanted to climb out of sight, where no-one could watch. Did she feel the need some time to not be Martina? To just be? But she'd called it work. Was climbing work for her now? Had the ballet become work? He'd assumed it was fun, or release, or something, anything but work. The way his writing had been a release, before it had been work. And, she was going to stay here for a while. A long while. Even through the rainy season, which he knew was at least a month away, though the first foreboding thunderstorm had rumbled back in the mountains just the day before. So much to parse, so much information in just one sentence.

"Parada," Martina exclaimed. "Hold us here."

Kane thought back to Boy Scout camp at Algonquin Park, and then to fishing with his sister. Circled his paddle the way his Ojibwa teacher had taught him, in alternating little circles to hold them in place with the gentle rise and fall of the still calm waves. The old motions were still with him as he felt his little power merge and blend with the big power of the water.

"Mas cerca, closer to the rock," she said. The gleam of her flashlight worked up the rock face, slowly, ever so slowly. As it rose, her hands and feet and fingers and hips worked a delicate pantomime, trying a first position, then a second, without ever leaving the kayak. Kane watched in fascination, witnessing the first ascent, the real first ascent, that happens before hand or foot ever touches rock.

Minute after minute spun out as the gleam of the flashlight rose higher, then onto the ceiling. Without being told, Kane positioned the kayak under the beam. As her gaze reached the opposite face, where the arch started back towards the water, he moved them in closer, felt where she was looking, turned her as she turned her hips.

"Thank you," she said, turning towards him, beaming.

"No. Thank you," he answered.

"For what," she asked.

"For sharing that with me. The first ascent."

"No first ascent," she said. "Maybe no ascent. Is mas difficile."

"You will try it?" he asked.

Martina weighed her words, considered, flashed the beam back up this face, over the arch, then down the first face.

"Si," she said. "But not today." "First we drill a bolt for tying the boat. You paddle for me. You belay me from the boat? After I drill?"

"Si," he answered.

"Don't answer so fast. Is hard work. Hours holding the rope while maybe I move, maybe I no move. And no climbing for you. Just the rope."

"Still yes," he answered.

"Porque?" she asked. "Why you do that for me. For me you just met?"

Kane had no immediate answer, realized it was an excellent question.

"Porque?" she asked louder, demanding.

"To see it. To see you. Maybe to be part of it?"

"A part of it? You want a part?"

"No. I don't want a part. I want to see it, to be a part. Not take a part, but to be a part. It's different. But yes. Si. A first ascent. Watching, enabling someone to do what is hard. Hard for them, yet worthwhile for me."

Martina considered his answer.

"Many want a part of it. So they can take. Take a little piece of me," she answered.

"Si," Kane answered.

"You take?"

"You give?"

"You know about the taking. You must. From when you wrote. Now you give all the time. When you doctor."

Kane slowly moved the paddle, trying to hold their place, trying to buy a moment of time to answer.

"So. You take? What do you take?" Martina asked.

Kane looked at the rock, at the water, at Martina.

"I take a memory. To be right here, right now. To see you move, and maybe to think of how to describe it, in my own words, so I can remember it when I'm not right here, and you're not right there, and I can't see you where you are. So that I don't take anything from you, but create something new, something we can both have that neither would have otherwise. To add, not subtract, and to be happy with the little addition."

Now Martina considered his answer. Weighed it, balanced it. Thought through all the answers she'd received to that question over the years.

"Bueno," she replied.

She pointed the flashlight back to the first face. She scanned back and forth, back and forth.

"Wait," Kane said. "Go back. Over there."

Martina obeyed. Scanned the beam back where Kane pointed.

"Oh my God," Kane managed. For there in the beam, subtle, but undeniable, was a painting on the rock, and words.

"Do you see it?" Kane asked.

"Si," Martina answered. "What is it?"

She played the light over the art as carefully as she had over her new route. Kane used every memory trick he had to try to fix the image more permanently in his mind. In his good mind. In the mind that had remembered every bone and vein and nerve and received a perfect score in anatomy and every other memory class. In the mind that remembered verbatim practically every word he'd ever written, and that could recall each of them, a task that was equally painful as it was impressive. In the memory that recalled each injury of each patient when they returned for their follow-ups, days, maybe weeks later. In the mind that every day froze him for at least a moment with an image from his wife's decline, a grimace, a swelling, a discoloration, a loss. In the mind that remembered harsh words, accusations about her passing. In the mind that sought to memorize these moments with Mina, nearly desperate to remember them for the certainty that they could not last.

"You have a camera?" she asked.

"No. No camera."

"Can you read it?" Martina asked.

"I was just about to ask you that," Kane said. "Isn't it Italian?"

"Not Italian. Like Italian. But not Italian."

Kane studied the words more closely. Then something in that mind clicked.

"Latin. It's Latin," he said.

"Latin?" Martina asked.

"Romans. Old Italians."

"Like the old men who I stay with?" Martina asked.

"No. Romans. Julius Caesar, Tiberius, Marcus Aurelius, Plinny, Caligula, Nero. Romans."

"Romans. Caesar. Si," Martina said.

Once again Kane worked his memory tricks and tried to parse the now recognizable Latin.

"A picture on the rock?" one of the old brothers asked Martina.

"Si."

"Graffiti?"

"No. A picture. And words."

"Words?"

"Si," Martina said.

"Kids," he snorted. "They should leave the old places alone."

"Kids who write in very precise and very old Latin," Kane said.

"Latin? Not Italian?"

"Si."

"I call Mario. You show him. He knows about these things."

"Mario?"

"Si."

Mario

"You are fit si?" Mario asked. "And climbers si?"

Martina and Kane both nodded, unable to speak as Mario's car whipped and slipped around hairpin turns on the roller coaster single lane path that was carrying them deeper and higher into the steeper and more barren mountains. Mario appeared unconcerned about the road, having taken two loud and long phone calls with, apparently, two different Italian women, both of whom were angry and loud enough to be heard over the squealing wheels and pounding heartbeats.

When his phone rang for the third time, Martina snatched it from Mario, opened it, and informed the caller that Mario was very busy driving on a very dangerous road and couldn't talk right now because he had to focus on the narrow, winding, dangerous road on which he was driving much too quickly.

Mario slid the car to a stop. He held out his hand to Martina, palm up, who returned his phone. He exited the car and dialed frantically. After a lengthy and animated call he returned to the car, outside of which Kane and Martina stood waiting, stretching muscles that had been tightened by the return trip in the kayak to the cave with Mario to see the pictographs and now by Mario's traversal of the twisting, narrow road.

"I sorry," Mario said. He made a show of powering down his phone and storing it in the trunk of his small car.

"I sorry," he repeated. "These women. They cause me so much pain," he started. His hands briefly came together over his heart. His pout would have been at home on the face of the most insolent three year old known to man. Though he had finished his degree and was now Professori Mario, anthropologist of all things old and Sardinian, the pout did not seem out of place.

Kane and Martina looked at each other, then motioned for him to go on.

"I tell you while we walk."

He grabbed a rope bag and his pack, then waited for Martina and Kane to pull their gear and packs from the car.

"This way," he said, and started off up into the rugged, dusty countryside.

Mario began, "never date sisters…"

"It is just up here, what I have been telling you about. I always remind myself to remember these were people once." His look and words were telling them "respect, don't touch."

"What's here?" Kane asked.

"People from the time of the drawing in the cave," he said. "You see."

First Martina, then Kane climbed the last few feet to the ledge on which Mario was perched. They clipped into his anchor, re-arranged their climbing gear, and let their eyes adjust to the light in the cave.

"Are those bones?" Martina asked.

"Si," Kane whispered.

Martina made a sign of the cross and cast her eyes down.

Kane's medical mind was already cataloguing the bones, deciding between male and female, determining age. His encyclopedic anatomical knowledge was tickling over forensic details.

"What you see doctore?" Mario asked.

"Two girls, young girls, and an adult."

"Young girls? How you tell?"

Kane launched into a lengthy and learned discussion of widths and ratios and orientations, most of which Professori Mario appeared to follow. But then, as Kane saw the pouty face returning with a vengeance, he realized his forensics had overrun his anthropologist guide. Neither noticed that Martina had moved closer and closer to the miniature skeletons, while growing quieter and quieter.

"If you have a photograph that we can enlarge, I can show you when we get back to town," Kane finished.

"Photograph. Si. I have photograph."

"I'm curious Mario. Why isn't this site better marked, part of a preserve? Or guarded? Or why aren't these bones and their story in a museum?"

Mario nodded his head knowingly.

"Is complicated, but not so complicated. I find these bones two years ago. While climbing, while still a student. I think these bones mean something that my professori would not like. Same with the cave, and the picture, and the Latin words you find. I think these bones tell a story unlike the story of my Professori's research. So I no tell my Professori. Then I think maybe I tell museum. But when I talk to some people about the museum they tell me bad things. That many things that go to the museum go somewhere else. Like to the private collection of some rich man. Like Fabrizzio who arrives today. Even to Ebay! So I no tell the museum. I leave them here until I find a good Professori and a good museum. They here for two thousand years, a few more years no matter. I show you and Martina, because you show me the picture, and the Latin words. I think maybe there is a connection between your pictures and these bones. Maybe you two, together, are supposed to find these things here, to make this connection. Maybe yes, maybe no. But for now, until I know, and write my own paper, I share this secret with you, and no-one else, and I promise to keep your secret, and hope you will keep mine."

Kane nodded in understanding, knowing too well the intricacies of academic politics. Martina nodded slowly, vaguely.

"Two girls?" Martina asked slowly.

"Yes. Two young girls," Kane said. "And an adult. Probably a woman, but I can't be so sure as I am about the young girls. I will need to measure and think. Maybe send a fax to a colleague in the medical examiner's office in Toronto."

"Two girls," Martina repeated, the words barely a whisper.

Then Kane realized what he had done. How he had given his complete medical opinion right in front of her, in her ear practically, in his lecture room doctor voice, had forgotten for a moment about Martina's memories.

He took her hand, drew her back from the bones, and looked at her.

"I'm so sorry Martina," he said.

She kept his hand in hers, blinked away a tear, and motioned for Kane to get rid of Mario.

"Mario? Can you give us a moment here by ourselves? You know we won't disturb anything, but we'd like just a minute with them alone."

Mario looked at Kane, then at Martina. He noticed the glaze in her eyes and knew, without knowing why, that he should leave them alone.

"Si. I abseil now. You come down when you are done. Take

your time. I look around. Maybe find more caves, more people."

"I'm sorry," Kane said.

"No, I sorry Kane. I sorry you see me so sad. Like this. Here in this beautiful place, this amazing place. You know why I cry?"

"I think so. Yes."

"You know so much Kane. Too much?"

"I don't think I could ever know too much about you," Kane said.

Her hand still in his, she drew him closer, then closer still.

"You know me just a few weeks. You only think you know why I cry. You cannot possibly know. No-one knows. But, I tell you. I tell you now. Like you tell me. And maybe like happens to you, maybe you no want to be with me."

As she began and worked methodically through the untold facts of her story, Kane kept her hand in his and for once was thankful that words sometimes escaped him.

"The shadows are longer," Martina said.

They had been silent for an eternity following her story. He had never let go of her hand.

"We go. Mario must be impatient to go."

"Si. And I don't look forward to riding down that road in the dark," Kane added.

Martina reached into the cave and gently pulled a small rock from right beside the neck of the largest skeleton.

Kane said nothing.

She touched it, and turned it, looked at it so carefully. A hole ran clean through the gem.

She held it up to Kane.

"It's beautiful," Kane said.

"Is our secret," she said. She reached behind her and unclasped a thin gold loop that lay softly around her neck. She blew on the stone, then threaded the gold chain through the hold in the gemstone. It lay gently on her chest, just below her throat. Kane closed the clasp.

Hiking

Once again the early morning fog lay in folds and layers above the harbor. Above, from the rooftop garden at his hotel, Kane could look out above the fog and see the high peaks seemingly adrift in the sea of cloud. Checking his watch for the tenth time, he decided it was time to go. His hiking boots clicked on the old stone steps as he made his way down from the roof, then down his street, to meet Martina on the damp cobbles below.

"Today no boat," Martina said.

"Works for me," Kane answered.

"We walk."

"Is it far?" Kane asked.

"You see," she answered. And once again Mina lead off, setting the pace, knowing that Kane was following, doing his best. Knowing that he could never keep up, and knowing that he might kill himself trying.

They walked towards the harbor.

"I thought you said no boat?" Kane asked.

"You see," she answered.

They walked past the boats, past the harbor, and past the last few brightly colored buildings in the town. The infinite ocean stretched out before them, and the limestone mountains rose to their left. Oleander grew alongside the road that turned to path as it took them further from town. The path ended abruptly at a cliff that hung precariously over the warm Mediterranean below.

Martina slowed, stopped, turned to Kane.

"I go slow here, so you see where I put my feet. Is tricky for a few feet, then there is a good path."

Kane looked at the ocean, the mountain, the cliff, and then Martina. Waves crashed into the rock below them, sending the lightest of mists floating up the cliff to glisten and make tiny, fleeting rainbows in the morning light. She tightened her pack, which was as heavy as his, maybe heavier, and began a slow traversal off the end of the path and onto the cliff. Kane watched where she held, watched where she stepped, until she disappeared around a bulge.

"Now what?" he muttered.

Martina's tanned face peaked back around the corner. A few

stray blonde hairs had escaped her pony tail and momentarily flew free in the salty breeze. Kane became rooted for a second, different reason. How she took his breath away, how he reacted. Though he had loved his wife, unquestionably, undeniably, and completely, there had never been moments like this, when he could neither breath nor speak.

"Vaya. Slowly. Is not so hard Kane. Just these two moves. I promise."

Kane grabbed where she had grabbed, stepped where she had stepped, tried not to look down at the ocean some eighty feet below, where it crashed onto the tangle of car sized boulders, and followed Martina around the bulge. Just one foot further and the path she promised stretched out before them.

"See? Not so hard Kane."

"Si," he answered. "Mina?"

"Yes?"

"You always walk ahead, and so fast. Today, can we try? Maybe, you walk beside me?" He wondered if it was asking too much to ask her to slow down. Wondered if he was asking her to compromise. Hoping he would never ask her to compromise. Hoping that he could eventually reach towards her, and not be such a drag.

Martina smiled, tilted her head to the side, and held out her hand.

"You hold my hand, then I no walk too fast," she said.

"It will be slower," Kane said.

"Si. But maybe some journeys together should last a minute more."

Kane smiled, took her hand, and fell into step beside her.
Mina's touch, above the waves, on my hand. More words.

Like the trip back over the mountain on the day they met, not two words passed between them. Here and there one or the other stopped to take in the vista spreading out before and above them. A water bottle was offered and taken, a small piece of chocolate shared, but still no words were spoken. Yet the understanding between them grew, and a few more words, a few more lines, were added to the poem that was forming in Kane's mind. It was always that way. A word, a few words, then the forming, and tumbling, and re-arranging, and then it sprung out fully formed. A release, and an exhaustion. Complete and pure and exhausting and liberating all at once.

The air was cooler here at the end of the path where a large amphitheater of limestone opened towards the sea. This rock was smoother to the touch, rounded, sloping, with no edges. It was not the sharp and featured limestone of the rugged inland mountain. Instead, it felt almost soft to the touch. It asked to be caressed. The incessant seaside breeze and the constant seaside moisture had smoothed away the rough edges. This would not be an easy place to climb.

"This first route is easy for me. Maybe not so easy for you. I climb it a few times, up and down, then you climb it while I rest, then I try my project. Si?"

"Si," Kane answered.

Martina readied herself while Kane readied the rope and the gear. He spread a small tarp near the base of the climb, then carefully flaked the rope, checking it for nicks and cuts and flat spots. He worked with surgical precision, and with a care for the health of his new friend. He watched her stretch, clean her shoes, chalk her hands, visualize the route. He watched her tie her knot, double checked the knot, and took his position to hold the rope. "I no fall here, but I let you hold the rope because I know you like the rope," she said.

"Gracias," Kane answered.

"And so I teach you. Not too tight, not too loose, so you can catch me, but so I no think about the rope."

"Gracias," Kane repeated.

"Why you thank me?" she said.

He thought of the time Wayne Gretzky had needed stitches after an exhibition hockey game in Kane's town. Thought of how Gretzky had told him to come out to the rink the next day so he could thank him for the stitches. Thought about how Gretzky had shown him how to flick the puck just so. Such lessons from such masters. That's why he thanked her.

"For the lesson," he said.

"Da nada," she said, not understanding. Then she was off, slowly at first, maybe even stiffly, for her. He saw a short, brutal scar on her right Achilles. Even so, she was fluid and liquid and powerful all at the same time from his and any other point of view. As she climbed up and down he saw the years and the injuries and the day to day things drop away from her one after the other. Saw her movements go from mechanical to instinctual. He saw her shed her vertical world, and as she did, felt her leave him behind in his. Though they were tied onto the same rope, he knew that while she climbed that rope did not connect their lives, could not span their worlds. That it separated them more than it joined them. He suspected that theirs would be worlds that intersected, maybe beneficially to both, but that would likely only intersect. He wondered if he could be satisfied with the momentary intersection, or intersections. Prayed that he could. Realized that although he could understand a part of her world, maybe better than most people ever could, that he could never completely understand her world, her physical mastery, and the intensity of her loss. His new found love for Mina had caused him its first poignant pain. He double checked his hold on the rope, and cast his eyes back up to where she climbed.

Her warm up route was 'maybe no so easy' for Kane. After Mina had climbed five laps on the warm up route, she had taken a drink and tilted her chin at the route, silently ordering her climbing partner to give it a whirl. As she lifted her chin to point again Kane saw the brilliant red rock on the glistening gold around her neck. Her eyes tracked his towards her neck, toward her breasts. She touched the rock with one finger, then tucked it back inside her top, made him look away.

"Remember Kane, look at your feet, pick where you will stand, then stand there. Put down your foot, then no move it. Dance on the rock, precisely, with respect."

He approached the rock.

"You need chalk?" she asked.

Kane caught her eye, and the devilish glint hidden therein.

"You think I need chalk?" he asked.

"Is okay if you need chalk," she said.

Kane reached into her chalk bag, brushed both his hands against her bottom, and once again approached the rock.

Kane tried to heed her words, and felt once or twice that he followed her words, as he slowly worked his way up the route. After fifty feet or so, he could go no further.

"Lower," he called down.

"Better," she stated as he sat panting, bathed in sweat.

"Grazi," he managed.

"I stretch while you rest, then, I work. You hold the rope. Not too tight. Too tight is no good. Too tight no count."

Kane considered that her statement likely applied equally to both the rope and to her. Considered that any rope that held any tension would be too tight for her. Knew that while the presence of the rope could give her the chance to express herself completely, also knew that the fact of the rope could destroy the expression. Knew that even an awareness of the rope would be too much.

"And no talk. You let me concentrate. So, no talk, unless I ask you. Okay?"

The conditions for the outing kept multiplying, but Kane agreed, vowed to be true to his word, to try not to take, to think of how to add. These were the first spoken conditions. So far he had adhered to the unspoken ones. But now the contract was laid out more clearly. She was here to work, and so was he. It was work he understood, and conditions he accepted.

She began to work her project. Up, up, down a bit, up a bit, back down, back and forth. Searching, puzzling, working, discovering, never weighting the rope. Resting where she could, advancing then retreating. Kane tried to hold on just tight enough, not too tight, to be there without really being there, to be unobtrusive. To blend, maybe to merge. No, 'merge' wasn't right. Intersect? Overlap? Orbit?

Orbit was the word that fit.

He thought to himself that he might never be able to fit into her world. Might never become part of her world. But he became certain he could orbit at the distance she would allow. He thought he might want to try, for whatever minutes, and routes, and days she would share, to be part of her world. And maybe, as he held the rope and watched her go up and down, up and down, he thought that she might fit somehow into his. Not his emergency room world, not that cold world in northern Canada. Not that world of slap shots and stitches and junior hockey and moose and salmon runs and boreal forest. He knew she would not be part of that world, would not be part of any static physical world, but rather she could be part of his world of words, his world of vacations, his world away, his returning world of poetry and climbing and travel and laughter. A world where she could ascend the rock before him, a world where their planets in their orbits could momentarily affect each other, making a higher tide, perhaps a flood tide in a world where he might touch her one day. A world where she could always be just a word or page or touch away.

"Watch me here," she called down over her shoulder.

Kane bent his knees, checked the slack in the rope, and readied himself to catch her fall, if indeed she did fall. But she did not fall. She moved past the spot to which she had climbed a dozen times so far. She clipped the rope into the karabiner in the bolt on the cream and grey and streaked limestone wall and then let out a solitary whoop. She scurried a few more feet, clipped the anchor and called down "lower me Kane."

The rope slid smoothly through his Gri-Gri as she returned to his side.

He had never seen her smile so brightly, so freely, so completely. He knew at this moment that the climbing was not work, at least not today. That the climbing was part of her, was her joy, was who she was for those liberating moments. That this physical world of grace and power and beauty and motion was her world now, like the stage and the dance and the music had been her world before.

"It goes, Kane."

"Si," he answered.

"Grazi," she said. She kissed the air beside both his cheeks, then wrapped her hands around him and kissed him on the neck. "Is only the second time I do this, and the first time without falling, from the bottom to the top."

"Brava," Kane said.

She squeezed him tightly one last time, very tightly. So tightly he felt the stone on the chain around her neck press into him. A nugget of hardness in this hard yet impossibly soft and strong woman. He smelt the salt spray in her hair, mixed with the chalk and dust on her hands, and the sweet smell of her sweat from her intense effort. He took it all in, and gathered her just a tiny bit closer into himself. In a moment he would have kissed her. But then she stepped away. Not away from his embrace, but simply in the joy of her success. The flush of the send was still on her. She seemed younger, a woman without memories, a woman completely in her element and in her moment. A woman Kane knew for certain he loved, and a woman he knew for certain he could love forever, though he feared that love would not be the best thing for either of them. A momentary look of sadness flickered in his eyes. A flicker that Mina observed but did not register while savoring this delicious moment of success.

Kane mentally added more words: "Mina's touch, above the waves, on the rock, on my neck."

The sun had disappeared over the mountain by the time they had rested and gathered and repacked for the hike back to town. The climbing partners returned to the bulge at the end of the path. To Kane it appeared as some sort of portal, a dividing line between *here* with Mina and her effort and her perfection and his addition to her world, and *there* with Mina and everyone else and all those who would subtract and take. Once again she tightened her pack, looked at Kane, and told him to watch where she held, step where she stepped.

"Just a second," Kane said.

Mina stepped back off the traverse, stepped towards him.

"Si? What is it?"

"Before we get back, before everyone else is there, can I tell you something?"

Martina paused, nodded.

"I had a good day. Thank you. Thank you for sharing that work with me."

"It can be not much fun for you to hold the rope all day," she said. "Tomorrow we climb for you. I rest, I hold the rope for you for a while."

Kane somehow felt dismissed, belittled. Like she had missed his point. His point that watching her work was play for him, fun for him. That working with her was a good pure work. That being near that effort and beauty somehow made him whole and better and motivated to seek his own limits.

"That's not what I meant, but thank you," Kane started. "What I meant was, you don't have to. But thank you for the offer. It was enough to just be with you today, and to see you work, and to see you happy. I don't need you to hold the rope in return."

Martina's eyes clouded, and her mouth narrowed.

"You no want me to hold the rope for you?" she asked.

"You probably have better things to do," he said.

"Better things?" she answered. Her cheeks were flushing red, but unlike the flush of victory from the climb, it was an angry flush. "Better things?" she repeated, her voice rising. She took a deep breath, settled herself. "Kane. I think you a good man. I think you different. I happy you hold the rope for me today. You a good partner. A partner, not a slave, not one of these people on the beach who ask for autograph. I want someone to hold rope, I find anyone. I no like it, but I find someone. You see what the people are like when they see me. I think if you want someone to get you a pencil and a paper that you have no problem. But you no like it. I know you no like it. I think you want to write at peace, maybe alone, maybe with a friend. Not with a, how you say, groupie? So I no offer to hold the rope to pay you back. I no offer the rope because I want you autograph. I hold the rope for you because I know you like to climb too, and because I want to be with you, to see you move, to see you enjoy it, to maybe help you get better. To work with you like you work with me. Work together at something we both love. Like when you asked for the lesson at Dorgali. If you no want me to hold the rope, you say so for you, not because of what you think I want. I say what I mean, I tell you what I think. You no think for me. If you no want to be with me, you say so. But I think you want to be with me. I see it in your eyes, I feel it when we walk together and no talk."

"I want to be with you," he said.

Martina raised his hand to her lips, kissed it gently, then disappeared around the bulge.

Dinner

Moonlight.
Gentle Mediterranean breeze.
Subtle scents and flavors and thoughts.
White wine, Pinot Grigio.
Fresh fish. So fresh it was swimming that morning, maybe even that afternoon.
Fresh pasta. Cavatelli. Cavatelli that had been semolina, water, and salt just hours before.

Martina and Kane sat in the glow of the day's climb, of the day's togetherness, of the day's understanding, on the stone patio at the hotel Cala Luna. The patio clung to the cliff above the harbor. The moon had risen slowly, full and pregnant with the night.

They were seated in the corner, under the oleander, away from the narrow cobbled street that separated the patio from the hotel. Around them the other guests nibbled, drank, talked, and likewise soaked in their own little piece of paradise. The discrete staff, who knew who they were, both now and in their other lives, served and smiled and treated them just like any other guest. For which they were grateful.

For 'the word' had gotten out. That Martina was here climbing, that Kane was here writing, and that somehow they were "together". Each was news, together it was big news. Tabloid news. They held hands across the table as the last dinner dishes were cleared away.

One man, who had clearly been waiting patiently, seized the moment of the dishes being cleared to approach them and ask for an autograph. Martina signed and smiled what Kane called her "public Mina" smile. Then the man handed the paper and Sharpie to Kane. Kane signed and delivered what Martina called his "go away" smile. As the man inhaled to speak, Kane dismissed him with a "nice to meet you" that left no doubt he had been dismissed. The man left.

The first autograph lead to a second. Martina sensed Kane's growing discomfort.

"Do you want to go up? To the rooftop garden?" she asked.
"Si," Kane replied.

They pushed back from the table, weaved their way across

the patio, and stepped out onto the cobbled street.

"Martina Fucentese?" they heard a girl's voice from the side. An excited voice. "Is that her? That's her. I swear it is."

Martina's hand tugged against Kane's as she stopped and as he took another step across the street.

"Martina! Hi," the girl smiled so nervously and fully that Martina simply had to stop and talk, could not just walk away.

She waited, smiled, listened for the pleasantries. Nodded politely. Her hand slipped from Kane's. He continued across the street, looked up to the garden, and took the first step into the hotel. But then he stopped. Turned. Thought about adding and not subtracting, about orbiting, about taking this part along with the rest. About being there for it all, not just what he wanted, not just what he craved. About giving her the support she might want in this moment, and others like it. So he turned and walked back. Took up position beside her. Touched, but did not hold her hand.

Martina turned almost imperceptibly towards him, grazed his hand with hers, and smiled a private smile for him. A little "thank you".

"Did you climb today?" the girl asked.

"Yes. A small project I've been working on. Nothing major."

"Nothing major?" Kane said towards her. "Wasn't it..."

Martina turned and silenced him with her eyes.

"Wasn't it what?" the girl asked Kane.

"Isn't it funny how a little training day can seem like something major to you and I?" he directed at the girl.

"For sure," the girl said.

"Will you take a picture with me?" the girl asked. She handed her camera to Kane. "Will you take our picture mister?" she asked.

Martina stood beside the girl and smiled another smile that Kane had named, the "public picture" smile. Kane snapped the photo in the digital camera, snapped it again, satisfied with the second take, and handed back the camera.

"Thank you so much," the girl said. "I'm sorry I interrupted you. Thanks again, and have a great night."

Martina and Kane finished their walk across the street and into the hotel.

"You don't like it when people talk to you do you?" she asked.

"No."

"And you don't like to sign autographs," she said.

"No."

"Why?"

"I don't know. It just doesn't work for me. I don't feel like I can give so little."

"Little to you, not so little to them."

He nodded his reply, his assent.

"Why didn't you tell her about sending the project?" he asked.

Martina paused. She took a sip from her wine and looked out over the balcony to the moon and the sea and the night.

"Because it's not done yet."

Kane started to answer, to say he'd seen her finish. But he paused, waited, chose to listen.

"It's not done the way I want to do it yet. Top to bottom, in one go, no up and down, on lead. That's when it'll be done for me. And then after a while I'll tell my friend Fabrizzio and he'll put an update on his guidebook and then people will know that route has been climbed."

"And that you did it," Kane said.

"Who does it doesn't matter. It's only the doing. And how it's done."

Kane now sipped from his wine, took his turn looking at the night, at the moon, at the sea.

"I'm not sure I understand," he said.

"Yes you do," she answered.

"I do?" he asked.

"Si. Is like the poem in your head."

"The poem in my head?"

"Si. The poem about me."

"About you?"

"Si."

"How could you possibly know about that?"

"Kane, a woman knows when a man is in love."

"Am I in love?"

"Aren't you?"

"Yes."

"When you know you should not love me. When you know I cannot love you back the way you love me."

Kane accepted the pain of the public voicing of what he knew to be true.

"But you keep that poem to yourself. You don't share it. Not even with me. Though I show you my work on my route. Though I show you myself on the spire. Though I hold your hand and sit with you in public and sip wine with you in the moonlight. Still you no share."

"It's different."

Martina waited for the explanation, for the rationalization. Kane started…

Mina's eyes, where waves meet sky
Mina's touch, above the waves, on the rock, on my neck…

Kane stopped.

"Is beautiful," she said.

"But not done," he answered.

"No. Not done," she answered. "Like my project. The moves are done, but the piece is not done. And so we hide our work, and then maybe, maybe when we are done, if we are proud with the doing, if we can live with the examination and interpretation, we share."

"Si," Kane said, as he stood beside her, on the rooftop garden, as the moon climbed ever higher in the Mediterranean sky, and as any doubt that he was in love, any doubt that may have appeared from the stern words at the end of the path dissolved into the gentle scents and gentle breeze and gentle love in the Italian night.

Swimming

Martina's feet touched the ground.

"I'm hot," she said.

"You've been working hard, and... yes you are," Kane answered.

Martina considered his smirk, smiled at his terrible flirty pun, and reached for the water bottle he handed her. She took a pull, wiped the glow from her brow, and pulled her pony tail back together. A bright flash of red erupted from the stone around her neck.

Kane's eyes were drawn from hers to the stone.

"Is beautiful si?" she asked.

"Si."

"And sad, because it reminds me of those girls in the cave."

Kane had no reply. He thought about tearing the stone from her neck and throwing it into the ocean to make that moment of pain he saw on her face go away. He did nothing.

"You saw the beach from the top of the cliff?" Martina asked.

"Yes."

"We go past it on the way out. We swim?"

"I didn't bring my suit," Kane observed.

"Or me," Martina smirked.

"I'm in," he managed through his suddenly constricting throat.

"Is a good shade of red for you," Martina teased.

Kane turned an even darker shade of red as his cheeks blushed even brighter.

A dozen people were scattered on the rocky, sandy beach. Two or three more were just in the blue, green, and white water, just at the edge, barely in to their knees, being bounced around by the waves. Half were naked, the other wore Italian bathing suits, and thus were substantially naked. The surf was steady and rough. Martina dropped her pack by a boulder ten feet from the high tide line. Kane put his beside it.

"You first," she said.

Kane hesitated, saw that she meant to watch him undress, and turned his back.

"Kane, I am over here," she said.
"Nobody wants to see this," he answered.
"I see you sooner or later, no?"
Kane turned back towards her.

He pulled his Dri-fit top over his head, folded it neatly, and placed it on his pack. She tapped her foot lightly, imitating impatience. Kane dropped his trousers, folded them neatly, and placed them on his shirt.

Martina continued to tap her toe.

"Oh for the love of Pete," Kane mumbled.

"I first see now, before the cold water, or after," she said.

"I get your point," he said.

Kane pulled down his boxer briefs, folded them, and put them under his pants.

Martina smiled a small smile of approval, then turned her back and disrobed in an instant. She flung her clothes towards her pack and ran for the water.

"Vaya," she said.

Kane stepped gingerly on the hot rocks and the even hotter sand. Dancing from left to right he finally arrived at the water's edge where Martina waited for him. She took his hand, looked right into his eyes.

"Kane, to you this is different, maybe sexy. To me, this is every day, but not quite so every day. Because it is with you, and you are nervous, and not so every day. To me, this is just the way things are. You want me to relax? To have fun si? So please just have fun. Swim. Siesta. Don't think of me as 'sexy naked Martina'. Please don't think of me that way. Because you know that is not who we are. Do what you said you would try to do. Think of me as just Mina."

"I'll try," he said. "But it will be mas difficile because, there's no other way to say this, it's simply an objective fact, you are the most beautiful, most amazingly beautiful, sexiest person I have ever seen."

Then he blushed again. Partly at her nakedness, partly at his, but mostly at his torrent of words.

She blushed in turn. But shyly, even for her nakedness.

She kissed him on the cheek, turned, and splashed deeper into the water where a crashing wave instantly pulled her ten feet into the ocean. Kane followed, surprised by the power of the undertow so close to the shore.

The cool water was clear. It embraced him, supported him. The salt water was so dense he could float effortlessly on his back, rising and falling in the ocean swells beneath the never ending Mediterranean sun. The water was so clear Kane could see hundreds of fish darting in and out of the boulders strewn on the bottom. Silver fish, blue fish, long narrow fish. Sea grass stood and swayed on the ever changing current. Seeing an especially colorful fish, he tipped up, kicked over, and propelled his once-upon-a-time lifeguard self down towards the bottom. One, two, three strong strokes seemed to bring him no closer to the fish or to the bottom. He stopped, looked back at the surface, and pulled towards it. Breaking clear he gasped for air.

"Where did you go?" Martina asked.

"I saw a fish. Went for a look. It's really deep here."

"Maybe we should go in closer?" Martina asked.

For the first time Kane looked back at the shore with the appraising eye of that long ago lifeguard. He realized the tide must have slowly been pushing them out to sea while they frolicked in the sunshine as he drank in her beauty. The analytic inside him assessed the situation and roundly chastised the frolicking absentee doctor.

"Yes. Maybe we should," he said.

They started stroking, slowly but steadily overcoming the tide and wind and currents.

"Is a long time to go back," Martina said, slightly out of breath.

"Yes," Kane answered, noting her labored breathing.

"Mas difficile," she said.

"Yes. Just a little more," Kane answered.

They swam until they were no more than twenty feet from the shore. They still could not touch the bottom. The waves bobbed them up and down and inexorably back out to sea. Though she tried, she could get no closer to the shore.

"What's happening Kane?" she asked.

"It's the tide, the outgoing tide, and a rip current."

"I no swim much longer," she said.

"We should try over there," Kane said, pointing along to where the shore jutted out. "Vaya."

They pulled parallel to the shore, until they were even with their packs and the small point. Swimming across the current had pushed them a little further away from the shore.

"Kane. I swim no more," Martina said.

"You can float. It's so salty, you won't sink."

"But the waves, they are too strong. I no get through."

Kane knew most people who drowned in the ocean drowned just like this, very close to the shore. Exactly like this. Caught in and then exhausted by a rip. Common in Lake Superior, where the cold could take them so quickly. But even in Lake Ontario, at the Sandbanks, or at the Outlet, or even at North Beach, in the warm summer water, people died twenty feet from the shore.

"Martina. I'm going to go up on shore and then bring you the climbing rope. Just float here while I go. Then I'll pull you in."

"Don't leave me," she said, the first tremor of fear entering her voice.

"To get the rope I have to leave you. Now float, and keep your eyes on me. Only on me. Then grab the rope and don't let go. Don't ever let go."

Before she could protest, Kane pulled as hard as he could and caught the leading edge of a wave that surfed him up and onto the shore where he landed hard on the rocks on his shoulder. He stumbled to the packs, found the rope, and stumbled back to the edge of the sea. Two naked boys who were sunning themselves with their naked mother looked at him like he was crazy. In the thirty seconds he'd been gone, she'd drifted out five more feet.

Kane dropped the bulk of the rope at his feet, waded out to knee depth, and hurled a knotted end towards her. It splashed just short and out of her reach. He retrieved it as quickly as he could. The boys got to their feet and came closer to Kane.

He pulled out ten more feet of rope, coiled it in his hand, and threw with all his remaining strength. The knot in the rope soared directly over her head and splashed behind her. So fixed on him were her ever-widening eyes that she neither saw the rope nor felt the splash. He pulled it towards her until it lay across her shoulder.

"Grab on. With both hands," he said.

She did, and in that moment the largest wave of the afternoon washed over Martina and then a moment later knocked Kane from his feet, back into the surf. The two boys, understanding what they were seeing, latched on to the rope and began to fight the waves and the tide and the sea.

Kane stumbled to his feet, spit the water from his mouth, and struggled back towards the rocky shore. He saw the boys, told them to hold on tight. Together they held the rope while Kane pulled himself to shore. When Kane reached the shore he told the boys to walk away from the shore, to pull the rope, then he too started to pull. Martina's head dipped under the waves, then suddenly re-appeared, only a few feet from the shore.

"Stand up," he screamed.

She tried, lost her footing, and let go of the rope as another wave crashed over her head.

Kane jumped back into the water, into the surf, found her beneath the wave and pulled her the last few feet to the shore. They stumbled as the last wave tripped them and tumbled them down, just beyond the reach of the hungry sea. Martina's brow crunched against a larger rock on the beach, causing it to swell instantly.

Martina, exhausted, scared, and out of breath came to rest lengthwise on an equally spent Kane. The adrenalin that had given him the strength for the last act coursed and pulsed and pounded in his ears. As he caught his breath he realized that he was still naked and that she was still naked and that she was laying lengthwise atop him, holding him like the man who had literally just saved her life. He realized, as she did not, that he had foolishly put her in harm's way in the first place. That the peril from which she had been saved was of his own creation. Thought that perhaps this was how it would be for them. That being together would be dangerous, especially for her. He gently brushed her hair back from her face, looked directly into her exhausted eyes, not inches away, and held her more tightly than he had ever held anything or anyone ever before.

Neither noticed that both the chain and the gemstone were gone from around her neck.

Dreaming

Kane and Martina stood on the sidewalk outside her rooms. The possessive old Sardinian brothers competed for who could glare most menacingly at Kane. But he was oblivious to them today. Perhaps they were concerned about the swelling on her brow, and how it came to be there. Perhaps they just hated Kane for stealing one second of Martina's attention.

"You come in with me," Martina said. "Just for a while. I no want to be alone right now."

"Si," Kane answered, his guilt about the near drowning blinding him to the fact that the most beautiful woman he'd ever known had just asked him to come to her rooms. Guilt that he had compromised her trust, without her even knowing. Guilt because he'd felt the undertow and the rip the second they entered the water and had ignored it, distracted by the moment, distracted by love, and, in his most honest moment of self-analysis and self-loathing, distracted by lust. Equated that momentary distraction with the larger picture of them ever being together. He felt the danger, felt the tide, and yet waded in anyways.

During the entire walk back from the beach he kept thinking 'I should have known'. Guilt. He'd known guilt. Had even embraced it after his wife had died. Hadn't he been responsible for her death, at least in some way? Couldn't he have done more to save her? Shouldn't he have tried one more thing? Anything? Shouldn't God have taken him, not her? All the years of hurt and pain and agony had clung to him as guilt as they had slowly walked back to her rooms.

"I shower. You wait for me?"

"Si," Kane answered. He sat on the floor, slumped against the wall in the corner of her room farthest from the window. Buried in the shadow, buried. He'd buried his wife. On a frozen January morning. In northern Ontario. Surrounded by family and colleagues and friends, mostly hers, few his. On the coldest morning in the coldest week. So cold that the grave diggers had needed a back hoe with a pneumatic jack hammer to crack open the frozen ground because she had made him promise she would be buried and not wait out the winter in a mausoleum. Finally actually buried her, after burying her so many times in his mind during the many years of her "decline." Even now he could not name her killer, not even the doctor in him could compartmentalize her pain, or his, or his perceived culpability. Intellectually he knew he had done all he could, and that the disease was genetic, beyond his control or doing. Emotionally he knew it was his fault, just as today's near drowning was his fault. Guilt, again, and raw and fresh and now.

She saw him with his head down, in the shadow, and quietly crossed the room to stand near him.

"Kane. Is okay now. We okay."

He looked up at her, ached to reach out his arms and take her in and hold her and empty himself into her. To empty all those years of fear and the following years of silence and being alone. But his arms remained down, in the shadow. As they had remained at his side while the others had crossed themselves and prayed that frozen morning by the grave of his forever silent wife.

Martina leaned down to him, put her hand to his chin, lifted his face towards her. "Not so sad," she said. "I shower, you rest, on the bed. But not so sad."

She made him stand, removed his shirt, pulled back the covers, and made him lie down. She kissed him on the forehead. "Now rest," she said.

Kane sensed her in his dream. Martina? She was climbing into bed beside him. Judith? His wife? His lover? She was sweet-scented and warm from the shower. One arm was wrapping around him the way Judith had, the other tenderly brushing hair from his forehead in a way she never had. She was speaking softly. But the words were Spanish, or Italian, not French-Canadian. He thought she might be saying she was falling in love with him. He didn't know whether to wake up and answer or to try to keep this dream alive for as long as he could. The sweetest dream. The most awful nightmare. He slept.

He woke in Martina's arms.

"So it wasn't a dream," he said.

"Not a dream," she answered. "But a long long sleep. Get up. I am so hungry."

At the mention of food, Kane also realized he was starving.

"I can't believe I'm leaving your bed to eat. But…"

"You can stay in my bed if you like, but I am leaving because I am hungry and I am eating."

"Where did you put my shirt?" he asked.

"There," she pointed to the small table beside her bed. He paused to watch her in profile across the room as she arranged her hair. She was trying to make a few strands cover the bump from the rock. She had dabbed some makeup on the mark. Once again he felt himself smile a contented smile that was somehow wrapped up in her and here and them. Even with the near drowning, some happiness managed to touch him.

He reached for his shirt. Under the shirt he felt something hard, metallic. He lifted his shirt and saw that there was a picture frame beneath it. A handsome man in a bathing suit stood ankle deep in the water between two teenage girls, twins. Beautiful girls, not yet women, but on the cusp. Blooming, another cliché. Like their mother they were all legs and length and beauty. Dancers. Undoubtedly dancers. With eyes he knew would capture even those in the farthest rows. Like their father they were bronzed and brown-haired. They had her eyes, her cheekbones, his chin. He imagined Martina holding the camera, taking the picture, smiling as she captured the beautiful, playful moment. He imagined her picking through hundreds of frames to find just the right one to hold this picture. He imagined her packing this picture into her suitcase as she packed to travel, to come here, where she had met him. He wondered if the photograph was from the last day, before they had been taken from her. When Marcelo and Aurelia and Tatiana were taken together, leaving Martina without her husband, without her daughters, simply without.

His fingers lightly touched the frame, the glass. His eyes misted, and their images blurred.

"Did you find it?" she asked.

"Si," he answered. He placed the frame back on the table. He wiped his eye, which cleared his vision, took one last look at the three who had been taken, then put on his shirt.

She moved to the door.

"Andale. I hungry."

"Me too," he said, stepping towards her, towards the door.

They walked hand in hand from her rooms to his. The stone patio was quickly becoming "their place". The dishes the chef made from the impossibly fresh ingredients were easy to savor, hard to resist.

"It's a little chilly. Can I go up and get a sweater before we eat?" he asked.

"I come with you," she said. "Help you pick."

"Are you saying I have no style?" Kane asked.

"No. You have style. How you say, for a lumberjack. Maybe tonight you let me choose?"

"This one?" he asked.

"No. That one," she said. "With that shirt, and those pants."

Kane raised an eyebrow, but obeyed. He realized he was getting used to dressing and undressing around her. And to listening to her advice. Something that had never happened with his wife. So many nights together in the dark. Maybe never truly seeing? He thought about how often and poignantly those days and these days were intersecting.

Kane stood before her in the clothes she had selected.

"You go look. See for yourself," she said.

Kane brushed past his new fashion stylist to look in the full length mirror in the other room.

Martina looked around his room. On the table where she had been resting her elbow, she saw a pad and a pen. She tried not to look. Stepped away from the table.

"How you like?" she called into the other room.

"I'm not sure," Kane answered.

"Trust me," she said. "I know about these things. Is not great, but is the best you have."

"So you're saying a former ballerina from St. Petersburg who lived in Paris and then in Buenos Aries and Rome has more fashion sense than an emergency room doctor from Northern Canada?"

No reply.

She stepped back towards the table. Looked at the pad.

"Dear Judith," it began.

Martina read the first line, and then the second. Now it was her turn for her eyes to mist.

"Okay. Let's go," she heard from the other room.

Martina read one last line, then joined Kane in the other room, then out the door.

"Do you still love her?" she asked.
"Yes."
"Has there been anyone? Anyone since…"
"No. Not until now."

Poetry

Gentle candlelight spilled into the fresh Mediterranean evening, splashed onto crisp white linen, and sparkled on the crystal and silver and china on their table. A mostly empty bottle of wine stood between them. Martina's hand lay softly in Kane's as he slowly, purposefully, skillfully massaged her fingers, her palm, her hand. Martina's eyes were half closed, partly from the wine, partly from the moon, mostly from the sheer ecstasy of his touch.

"I imagine you have a very nice bedside manner Doctore Kane," she said.

"Mmm," Kane answered, a silent chuckle forming on his lips.

"Are you happy?" Martina asked.

Without stopping, without interrupting his touch, Kane looked up at the moon, then back to Martina. "Rarely," he said.

Martina curled her fingers around his. Made him stop for the moment.

"I mean right now. Here? Now?"

Kane held her hand.

"Si."

"Tell me. Tell me how it feels. Tell me like you were writing a story just for me."

Kane returned to his caresses, to his pressures, to his searching and feeling and healing of her hands and of his soul. She felt his mind engage in both the story to tell and the pleasure and relief to bring forth from both hands and words.

"It's been a long time since anyone wanted to hear how I feel," he started.

"Tell me," she said. "I want to hear."

"Forgive me," he said. "I'm happy. Not happy like in a good dream. But happy like after you've just woken up from a bad dream. A bad dream where you've lost something tangible but unknown. You feel the loss, but don't know what you've lost. And then you realize you're safe in bed, in your lover's arms, surrounded by all that's good and right and worth living for, and then you smell your favorite breakfast cooking, the scent brought in on the crispest fall breeze that holds the colors and scents of the most perfect autumn day ever and you know, know absolutely, that someone loves you and today will be a good day. Happy that the nightmare is gone and that a new day is beginning and that you know the difference between the two, having experienced both."

His voice trailed off and Martina felt the tightness in his hands. Felt him tremble. Realized the magnitude of what she'd asked, and knew the significance of his answer. She brought his hand to her lips, kissed it, looked out to sea, then into his eyes.

"Thank you," she said. "Now you write that down and give it to me and never say it again or show it again or share it with anyone else. Can those first new words be mine and only mine? Will you let me be that selfish in this one thing?"

"Si."

"Then let me ask one more thing. And don't be angry Kane. When you touch your patients you only touch one at a time. A few a day. But before, you reached the whole world. Touched millions. Many millions by what the librarian says. Made them think and feel and be better for at least a few moments. How can you settle for just one at a time? For so few?"

"It's not settling for less."

"Then what is it?"

"It's something real. It's not a fiction, or a fabrication, or some trick to make people who feel nothing think they actually feel something. It's real. When I suture a cut the bleeding stops and the wound heals. It's real, tangible, objective, knowable, known. When I reduce a fracture it heals, mends together, maybe even stronger than before. The other, it was never real."

"Don't say that."

"But it's true."

"It's not."

"Oh really? Then what about you? Aren't you being a little hypocritical here?"

"No."

"Really?"

"Kane I can't dance. You've seen the scar, know the injury. You know I can't dance."

"Maybe not at the Bolshoi. But it's still a dance, a ballet, what you do now. It's grace and beauty and freedom. Yet you hide it away and no-one sees it and no-one is moved and no-one dreams of the lightness and freedom you bring down from heaven to us mortals here on earth when you move."

"Stop Kane, stop."

He stopped.

Their hands separated, yet their eyes remained fixed in each other's. The waitress approached, felt the intensity of the moment, and withdrew without a word. After a moment Martina spoke very quietly.

"So now we know we can hurt each other," she said.

"Yes."

"So we no do that."

He took her fingers back in his and slowly, gently, started to rub them under the brilliant Mediterranean moon and the flickering candlelight. Her eyes slowly shut, and her head slowly rolled to the side until it rested on his shoulder.

The dishes were cleared, the ocean side terrace empty but for Kane and Martina. The manager had heard of the rescue at the beach, and patiently waited inside, quietly bringing glass after glass of local wine.

"Will you stay with me tonight?" she asked.

"Yes."

"And we can spend tomorrow together?" she asked.

"I don't think so," he asked.

"Because we fought?"

"No. Because I have something to do."

Martina waited for more. Waited. Evaluated. Felt for something in his words.

"Can I join you?" she asked.

Now Kane waited. Thought.

"Yes. I'd like nothing more."

Healing

Martina and Kane were shoehorned into his tiny Italian rental car. He started up the narrow winding road that lead away from the sea, away from the town, up the mountain, and back in time.

"We go to Dorgali?" she asked.

"Through Dorgali."

"Then where?"

"To a hospital, more of a clinic actually. I've been helping out there some while I've been here."

Martina turned in the seat to look at him more directly. He felt her stare but dared not return the look. Both hands gripped the wheel. Both eyes were glued to the ever more narrow road, now more path than road.

"The manager of your rooms thought you had a mistress. That your secret was a woman."

"My secret?"

"He do not know where you go all alone. And he knows everyone on the island. So maybe he not know everyone, or everything. He thought it was a woman. Somehow I didn't believe it."

"Is it so impossible to believe?" Kane asked.

She tilted her head to the side and smiled in a diminutive way that made him realize that it was quite impossible to believe.

"So even with this mistress, you still wanted to be with me?" he asked.

"I feel that you are a good man," she answered.

"Occasionally," he answered, accepting the smile and its truth.

She grew quiet as the path narrowed even more, now barely a goat track.

"Are they all so poor?" she asked.

"Yes," Kane answered.

"How did you even know this place was here?" she asked.

"Doctors With Passports," Kane answered. They know about places like this, and people like these, and they match them up with people like me."

"They are no many men like you Kane," Martina said.

Kane finished washing his hands. She handed him a towel. He dried.

"Remember last night? When you asked me how I can settle for one at a time?"

"Yes. I see it now."

"No. Let me finish. Because you were right. At least in part. Because it is settling. I touch one at a time. Maybe a dozen today. But it's instant and it's real. It's just a little fix, but it is a fix. For me it is little, for them it is everything. You were right. It's not the big fix. It's an escape. A healthy escape. Don't get me wrong. A good escape. So many of the others from that time are totally insane. Looking for the big fix and never finding it. I tried some of those things. They didn't work. This works. Every time. It fills the parts that are empty and gone, and there are endless people who need the fixing. With my writing, I touched millions, hundreds of millions if you believe the publishers, but only for a moment here and there. And the touch was just a touch, a wispy brush, a breath, nothing more, nothing lasting. Here, to these little children, the touch is forever and it's real and it's something they might not live without."

Martina stepped towards him, wrapped him in her arms, and held him so tight. She waited as he stood stiff and apart. Finally she felt his hands encircle her and his body relax then melt into hers.

"There's something I want to show you," he said.

"What?"

"You'll see," he said.

He took her hand in his and for once he lead the way. He lead her out the door, to the left side of the clinic, and then behind.

"Is large," she said.

"I've been trying to get all the way around," he said.

"Not on top?" she asked.

"No. I'm crazy but I'm not stupid."

She approached his rock, for that's how she thought of it, as "his" rock. She noticed the smudges of chalk.

"Whose chalk is that?" she teased.

"It's yours, only yours, I swear," he said.

The car slid to a stop on the rain slicked cobbles in front of her hotel. The late afternoon shower had made the drive down the mountain harrowing for both of them. She reached for the door handle, but then lingered.

"Will you walk up the shore with me?" she asked.

"After I clean up?"

"Yes."

The rain clouds had lifted as the sun had disappeared over the mountains to the west leaving reds and oranges over the mountains and looming approaching darkness in the east over the ocean. Martina and Kane walked hand in hand along the sandy, rocky shore. Her pants were rolled above her knees and his were soaking wet. They came to a flat rock that extended up and out over the waves. Martina scrambled up, then so did Kane.

She bent her neck side to side. Snaked her spine back and forth, then rolled her toes and ankles. Kane watched, picked up the rhythm, and started rolling his shoulders in time to hers.

Martina dipped into a Yoga pose, the Warrior. Kane followed as best he could. She flowed from pose to pose. Limber, strong, focused. Kane mimicked her, from pose to pose. She caught his movement out of the corner of her eye.

"Here, let me help you," she said. She lifted his arm a few inches, moved his hips more over his knees, inhaled and exhaled. He picked up her breathing pattern. Moved to another pose. Once again she adjusted here, adjusted there, with just the gentlest touch, the slightest pressure. Pose moved to pose as darkness engulfed them.

"Thank you," Kane said.

"I always have time for someone who will work," she said.

"Thanks."

"And you earned it, with those children. And with the other. With the apology."

"Martina."

"Now you wait, while I tell you something."

Kane said nothing.

"You lucky," she started.

"How so?"

"Because you find something to fill it."

Kane considered. Nodded.

"Yes. But so have you."

Martina took a deep breath. Released it in a sigh.

"Not really. Is good. And I like it. But it does not fill it all."

"Why not?"

"Because you were right. Because is just for me. Sure sometimes people see. Like the people on the beach. Or like you those days at Dorgali."

"You saw me the other days?"

She scrunched her mouth in a swallowed ironic smile, rolled her eyes.

"You were trying to hide behind a tree but you were staring with your mouth open. Yes I see you."

"Oh."

"Anyway. You right. Is just for me. I liked it on the stage. The music, the lights, the people. I liked knowing that for a few minutes I helped them all be free. That I was using what God gave me to do something uplifting, something that touched them."

She drifted off.

Kane thought, calculated, considered whether to say it.

"Did your twins ever feel that?"

Martina answered immediately.

"Yes. They both said they did. We liked to talk about it. When we were training, rehearsing. It kept us motivated to try and try again, to make each movement as light as it could be. To smile no matter how much the effort, the pain. Knowing the dance would set them free, and in turn set us free."

Again Martina drifted off.

Kane knew he had pushed into an area she hadn't visited in a while. Was surprised how freely she'd shared. Yet she had left their picture in plain sight. An invitation?

"How much do you miss them?" he said.

"You ask so much," she said.

"I suspect that from you I will ask everything."

Martina's face flashed the ageless expression that has confused and will confuse men forever. But as quickly as it came, it was gone, and her face once again became serious.

"I miss them every day. Every day I see them, talk to them,

know that they are right here beside me. I think sometimes they will need me to let them go, but they're not ready yet. They still have each other, and that will help them in their journey. But neither I nor they are ready for them to go just yet."

Kane also knew about loss, about death. He'd felt the same things, but spread over the years and years of the inevitable decline they'd been diluted, even as they'd been purified, distilled, and intensified. Martina's loss had been so sudden, so traumatic, and unexpected, while Kane's had been inevitable, and ultimately a relief.

"What next?" she asked.

"Pardon?" he answered.

"What is next question in interview?"

"I'm not interviewing you."

"You're not?"

"Okay. I suppose I am."

"So? What's next?"

"May I?"

"You didn't ask my permission before."

"I know I'm trespassing," he said.

"It's what you do," she answered. "You're a doctor and a writer. In both activities you insert yourself into other people's lives, into other people's bodies. Some for the time it takes to sew a cut, to set a leg. Others for the time it takes to create their world and manipulate them as you move them to your tune."

"You're mistaken, about the writing at least."

"Oh? Don't you make up the people? Make up the story?"

"Not really. It's not like that. It's more like I'm observing them. I think about who they are, and what they might do or be. Maybe I start them in an interesting place and/or an interesting situation. But then I'm forced to observe, to report, to channel what they feel, say, do, believe. They are who they are and they do what they do. I can't make them do anything. If I try, the whole thing stops. They rebel, and it's no good. So no, I don't really have all that much control."

"In that case you're both a trespasser and a voyeur," she said. "Constantly living only through someone else's life. Is that why you stopped? Really? Because you lost who you were, or maybe realized you weren't anyone at all?"

Kane tensed, froze.

He stared at her in disbelief.

"How can you say something like that?" he asked.

"Because you know about my girls, and about me, and talking about them helps. So I say it because I think maybe no-one else says it to you and maybe it is true and maybe it helps."

She stared into his eyes, daring him to look away.

"You know I'm falling in love with you, right?" he asked.

"Yes. And I know in the end it will hurt you. But is your choice. I can no stop you."

Kane took her hand and swung it gently as the moonlight drifted and glittered across the rippled Mediterranean. They talked as they walked, falling deeper, faster, and farther, hour after hour, further and further along the shore, until the first rays of the morning sun kissed the sky above the shore.

Ghosts

"Is this breakfast or lunch?" Kane asked.

"Is good and fresh. Does it matter?" Martina answered.

They sat in the sunny breakfast room, from which all but the latest diners had long since departed.

"I slept so well last night," Kane said. "And I'm not a good sleeper."

"Was it the yoga? And the night air?"

"Si, and si, and si."

"Is three answers. I only ask two questions."

"Two this morning, but you asked many more last night, questions no-one has asked me."

"Do I go too far?" she asked.

"No. Perhaps we should go further."

Martina savored a tiny piece of melon, a sliver of prosciutto, a morsel of cheese.

"Further how?" she asked.

"You know. Talking about what happened."

Martina placed down her fork, tilted her head to one side, then to the other. She closed her eyes, then slowly opened one.

Kane waited, wondered now whether he had gone too far.

"Yes, perhaps we should," she said.

She stood, took his hand, and led him towards the door, across the street, down the long flight of uneven stone steps that lead down to the rocky beach. She held his hand as she began an urgent walk away from the town, towards the path that lead to her project.

"I still don't know why they were kidnapped. Not for sure," she said. "There are many theories. Some say they only wanted money, but that makes no sense to me. If they wanted money they would have taken me and the girls, and made Marcello pay. He had the money, not me. Some say they wanted to make a political statement, that Marcello's business was doing wrong and needed to be punished. But that also makes no sense. Political statements are lost when the innocent are involved. And the girls were innocent. So I still do not know why they were taken."

"And the kidnappers were killed before they could be

questioned?"

"They all died together," she said. "The explosion took them all."

Kane had read this, knew how it had ended. Knew how the hostage rescue team had thrown a flash-bang grenade onto the ship where Marcello and the girls were being held. Knew that fumes from the ship's fuel tank had ignited, ending all their lives in a massive explosion that only one hostage rescue member had survived. Knew how that man had managed to apologize to Martina before he succumbed to his injuries. What he didn't know was how she felt. He thought that maybe no-one knew. That maybe this was her real gift to him, sharing something she had never shared with anyone else. And he knew there was going to be a price to pay. That to be honorable, and to be in love, he too would have to share. Share thoughts he had not thought, share words he had not spoken, share everything about Judith, the way Martina was sharing everything about Marcello and the girls.

"For a long time I no believe it," she said.

Kane sat and waited, held his questions, determined to just listen.

"They had been gone for a week already, and they had taken many trips together over the years. So I was used to being home alone. And I had travelled myself. So the quiet was known. But not this quiet. It was different. I no understand how, only that it was different. After a while I realized that the quiet was different because it was not going to end. And that the people who came by, people were always coming by, the people who came by were all sad. They were not looking forward to anything. They were not making plans for the girls, or for Marcello. They were making some plans for me, things I could do, but all the plans were just for me, or for me and them. There were no plans for the family. That's how the quiet was different. And Fabrizzio came to my home. He had never come to my home before."

With the talk of the quiet they had stopped walking. Their footsteps on the rocks seemed too intrusive. They stepped back from the shore, found a dry, flat spot on the beach, and sat.

She looked out over the water, but never released his hand.

"Then one day something changed. I woke up the same way as every day, I ate breakfast the same way as every day, but something had changed. I don't know what. I was different. I went to the girls room, like I had done every day, and instead of just standing and crying and looking through their things and laying down on their beds, I reached into their little dresser, where I knew they kept their journals. They both kept journals. They were both writers, like you, always with a pad and pen, or with a laptop. I took their journals, and went out in the back of our house, and began to read. Most of their words were just the little things you would expect of young girls. About boys, and dresses, and dances. But some of the things were unexpected. They were so observant. They said things about me and Marcello, things I didn't know they thought."

She paused.

Kane clinched his teeth down on his tongue to prevent the questions that were consuming him from spilling forth. He could not, would not, interrupt.

The waves whispered against the shore. High thin clouds whisked across the sky.

"It will rain tomorrow," she said.

Kane looked at the sky, clinched down harder on his tongue, unwilling to break her train of thought.

"It rained that day in the backyard," she said.

"So I went inside, to Marcello's office, and finished reading their journals. They were sad for me, because they thought the love between Marcello and I was incomplete, and impure. They suspected that I loved Fabrizzio. Not like I loved their father, but in some other way. Some way that I could not, or did not, love Marcello. In a way they did not approve. While I sat there in his office, with their journals in my hands, I realized they were right. It made me question my hurt, my loss. It made me understand the conflict inside me. I missed my girls, I missed them so much. I had cried so many tears for them, but not so many for Marcello. I realized how I had driven something between us, and now, when he was gone, I could never apologize, never make it right. Wherever he was, he was with the girls, and they were with him, and they all knew that I had betrayed them."

She stopped.

He felt her hand go cold in his.

Felt her wrestling the memory, seeing the girls and Marcello in heaven, seeing them without her, blaming herself that they were gone because she had betrayed them. And still Kane said nothing. The pain and suffering of hundreds of deaths in his emergency room had hardened him not one bit against the real death of his wife, and the invented emotions and dialogue of twenty one best sellers had not prepared him one bit for the real emotion of Martina's words. Kane swallowed hard, trying to just love her, to just be with her, to just let her be.

Gentle wave after gentle wave shushed in and out on the shore. They sat still in the lengthening shadows, felt the temperature change.

"Yes, it will rain tomorrow," she said.

"How do you know?" he asked.

"Because of the clouds, and the light, and the smells. It will rain."

"I trust you," he said.

"After what I just told you? How can anyone trust me?" she said.

"I trust you," he said. "With my heart, with my words, I trust you to hold the rope while I climb, in more ways than one I put my life in your hands."

"Why you trust me?" she asked.

"Because when you talk to me, you look me in the eye. You tell me the truth, without apology. You say the words you feel."

"Is that enough?"

"Is there anything more? Any better reason to trust?"

"Even after what I tell you?"

"Even so."

He felt the warmth return to her hand. Felt her pulse return to its strong, steady beat, felt the calm that settled on her.

"Will you tell me about Judith?"

Now Kane's hand went cold. He knew this was going to be the price. But he didn't realize how soon it would have to be paid. And how did she know her name? Form the library, of course. She said she had read about him, so of course she most know most of it already. And she knew what he had told her on the beach, after the sea spire. But, like she had, he had only told her the facts, the happenings. He had not shared his feelings about it. But that was what was now at stake. With her heart in his hands, with her confession and revelation still floating in the calm ocean breeze all around them, that was what was at stake. Not the what, or the how, or the where, or even the why, not the facts, but rather what it had done to him, how'd he'd felt, or not.

Kane let one more set of waves re-arrange a few more grains of sand, and let one more high thin cloud pass over head before he finally spoke.

"In the end it was a relief. The pain had been so much for her. It could have been less, I could have made it less, but she didn't like the medicine. Said it made her detached and stupid, and that she'd rather be sick than either detached or stupid."

He paused.

Martina thought that Kane was talking about Judith, and that she wanted to hear about Kane. But like Kane had before, she waited, gave him time to tell his tale in his own way. To give what he was going to give, not what she was going to extract.

"That's something I thought about a lot. I still think about it. How she didn't let the pain and the disease change her mind while it so insidiously changed her body. She'd been an athlete. A runner. Had won a medal in the Olympics. Her body was nearly perfection, until it turned against her. That was the cruelest irony, that this instrument of strength and speed and power that had carried her over the track in record times had turned so forcefully and completely against her, and yet took so long to break her. What had raced her forward, took its own God damned time and never killed her. Not really. Once, more than once, I asked her if she wanted me to help her. To help her...."

Again he paused.

Martina knew what he was trying to say, but knew he had to say it unbidden, without her prompting.

"To help her cross over. It would have been easy for me. I'm a doctor. I know what to do. I could have made her just painlessly drift away. But she always said no. One day I finally realized I wasn't helping. That she didn't mind the pain, or the sickness. That she accepted it. What she minded was people treating her like she was sick. On that day everything changed."

"I realized she knew she was going to die, but I realized she was still alive. In my mind I had killed her a hundred times. I had started living my life as though she was already gone. And that was the cruelest thing I could have done."

"She didn't want to be sick, so she was handling it by living. And I'd already started to move on, to live without her. So I stopped. I just stopped. She noticed right away. Noticed I was back with her, maybe more with her than at any other time. We made the best life we could, the two of us. It wasn't easy with all the doctors and nurses and everything. But we made it work. We went on like his for almost a year, while she deteriorated more each day."

"Then, then she started to say good-bye. In little ways at first, but then more overtly. She started to push me away. Like she thought it was going to be harder on me to live without her than it was going to be for her to die. Nothing had ever hurt so much. To have her push me away. But she was right. Oh my God was she right."

"Just like my first revelation, my first understanding, I didn't get this one right away. In fact, I didn't get it at all until she pretty much demanded that I start getting ready for 'after'. I told her I would have plenty of time for 'after', but she made me promise."

Kane paused.

Martina gripped his hand. Pleading with him to go on, to tell the promise, to finish the story. As she had finished hers.

"Then she asked me to leave the things out for her. So she could decide it on her terms. She didn't want me to have the memory of helping her. She just wanted me to leave the things out. So I did. And that morning, that last morning, she made me make one last promise.

"She made me promise to love again. Not to have a girlfriend, or to remarry, but to love again. She made me promise to love again, and to never compare.

"I've tried. Both things. To love again, and not to compare. But so far, until just now, here, I've failed in both. I have not loved. I've liked people, and gone on some dates. But I haven't loved. And I have definitely compared. Not you, well, not too much, but everyone else has been compared. So, I feel like I haven't kept my promise."

"But you have," Martina interrupted. Her voice was insistent, pleading.

"Pardon me?"

"You have loved. I've seen you with those children. You

don't love them the way a man loves a woman, but you love them more than a husband loves a wife. Because you get nothing back. You give, and give, and give, and you get nothing. So you have loved. And none of those children do you compare. You heal them, fix them, and they leave healthy. So there is no comparing."

Kane considered. Slowly, gently he rubbed his thumb on her hand, on her fingers. He brought her hand to his faced, kissed the fingers, drew her closer, kissed her on the left cheek, then on the right, then on her forehead.

For Kane this was, unquestionably, love. Love without compare.

For Martina, this too was love, pure and single love. Love without another intertwined. Love without an agenda. Love in a beautiful place with a good man. Love she knew he could not endure, and love that she suspected would destroy. For isn't that what she had always done? With the dance? And with Fabrizzio?

Kane drew her into his arms and held her as the waves whispered and shushed and as the thin clouds in the Mediterranean sky turned pink and salmon and red as day turned to evening, and evening to night.

Flood

"I've never climbed so much," Kane said.
"If you climb, you climb," Martina said.
Kane smiled, dipped his chin in happy submission.
"We climb," he said. "But you have to be back early for your interview right?"
"With Fabrizzio, and the sponsors, yes."
Kane cringed inwardly at that name. Fabrizzio. He had never met him, but already he didn't like him. Was jealous of him. Kane tried to push down the ugly jealous animal and to remind himself that it was him here today, not Fabrizzio.
"The sponsors, yes," he said.
Martina cinched up the strap on her pack, set out at her usual dominant feline pace, then, after a few steps, stopped, looked back over her shoulder, turned, and held out her hand. Kane stepped forward, took her hand, and they began at a more leisurely pace to walk away from the shore, up the canyon, towards the inland route Martina had chosen for Kane. Thailandia the place was called. He thought the name fitting as they worked up through the tangled brush and overhanging canopy in the oppressive humidity. As they followed the twisting path it started to rain very lightly, just a mist, barely noticeable in the incredible humidity. As the path narrowed, their hands separated, but Martina maintained Kane's pace.

Further from the shore the canyon narrowed and spread, narrowed and turned and spread again. The path went from rocks to sand to boulders and trees laying twisted at curious odd angles across the path. Hike turned to scramble that turned to bushwhack and back and forth with each turn. At one point they crawled on hands and knees through a tunnel beneath a pile of boulders. The light mist continued to fall.

"Adventure si? Like Indiana Jones?" she asked.
"Si," Kane answered. "Can we climb in the rain?"
"At Thailandia si. It overhangs. Rock is always dry."

"I think you will like this route," Martina said.
They were standing deep in the canyon, a mile from the shore, directly in front of a sixty foot limestone cliff. They and the entire route would have been in shadow if the sun had not

been obscured by the gathering thunderclouds. A trickle of water separated the walls of the canyon, which were at most twenty feet apart at this narrow point. The route was overhanging, severely overhanging in parts. The light rain, now more than a mist, fell on both sides of them, but not on them here in the rain shadow of the overhanging route.

"You think I can do this?" Kane asked.

"I don't know. We find out. But it suits your style."

"I have a style?"

"Si. You have a style. You fight the rock. Perhaps because you are strong. Very strong. In your hands, and arms, and back, and legs. Very strong. But not so balanced. This route is hard, even for someone strong. But it suits you."

Kane considered the analysis, trying to decide whether it was complimentary. He decided it was a simple recitation of facts from a master of the stone. So he tried to listen to the analysis, and act on it, rather than to react at a personal level. Analytical Kane triumphed over emotional Kane, and the analysis proceeded.

"What's your style?"

"Dancer. But today is about your style. Your climb. I hold the rope."

"Are you going to lead it first? Put the rope up?"

"No. Is your route, is too hard for me."

"Too hard for you? And you want me to lead it?"

"Si."

She began uncoiling the rope, finished, and handed the end to Kane.

"Si," she repeated.

The gently falling rain filled the air with scents and little sounds and made the overhang enclose them. Once again, they were completely alone, and together, and Kane could feel that this was who and where and what he wanted to be.

"Climbing," Kane said.

"Climb on," Martina answered.

He grasped the first hold with his right hand. The hold was large, and the edge was positive, almost sharp. His hand sunk deep into the limestone and felt secure. He looked over his shoulder, saw Martina holding the rope, a look of concentration on her face, and a playful smile. He matched his left hand with his right, adjusted both, then stepped from the ground to the wall. Instantly he felt the overhang, and he started to pull.

"Kane. No pull so much. Just hang, with straight arms. Feel the angle. Feel the rock. But stand on the rock, don't pull, stand. Be just strong enough. Look, and breathe, and then move."

Kane looked back at her, trying to parse the largest amount of instruction he had ever received in climbing. Perhaps more instruction than he had received in his entire time climbing.

"Is that all?"

"Si. For now."

He looked back at the rock, saw the next hold, reached for it.

"Kane stop. Put your hand back down, come stand beside me."

He obeyed, descended, stood beside her.

Martina looked him in the eye. Considered.

"Will you do something for me? Will you try?"

"If I can," he answered.

She nudged his foot with her foot.

"Will you move these first? Before you reach? Will you hold on and hold on and hold on, just enough, with your hands, while you let your feet move up and up and up? And only then will you reach?"

Kane looked at his feet. Looked in her eyes, reached around behind her and dipped his hands in the chalk bag hanging behind her. His hand brushed her behind while in the chalk bag. Deliberately. He brushed it again. He wasn't sure why he was doing it, why he was touching her behind through the chalk bag when he was here to climb, but he went on anyway.

"Kane?" she asked. "No chalk. Climb."

"If you remind me," he said.

He stepped back to the rock, grasped the large hand hold, and stepped back on.

"Climbing."

"Climb on. Move your feet first."

Her voice sounded right beside his ear. He could feel her breath. That excitement merged with his feeling for the rock. Her breath, warm, like the gentle rain that fell around them in the Mediterranean heat.

Foot, foot, foot, hand, hand.

Foot, foot, foot, hand, hand.

Foot, hand.

"Kane, your feet, you promised to try."

Her voice sounded a few feet away, but still close by, and insistent, instructing. Merging with the rain.

Foot, foot, foot, foot, hand, hand.

Foot, foot, hand.

Foot, hand.

"Kane, your feet, for me."

Her voice sounded smaller still, but insistent, and more a part of the canyon, of the air, of the place, of the showers.

Foot, foot, foot, hand.

Foot, foot, hand.

And then there were no more feet, only a hand hold, far above.

He looked down at his feet, looked some more, but there were still no feet.

"There's no more feet," he said.

No response.

"There's no feet," he said louder.

Still no response.

He looked back over his shoulder, and saw Mina standing fifty feet below, staring at him, insisting with her eyes, yet nearly beatific in her beauty and smile.

"There's no feet," he yelled.

She shrugged her shoulders, tilted her head, and gestured upwards with her chin.

Kane looked up, saw the anchors were just one long move away, and looked back at the last bolt he had clipped ten feet below. It would be a big fall if he came off now. But a clean fall, into space, because the cliff overhung the canyon so much at this point. Overhung so much that the now steady and more urgent rain did not touch the rope or the rock or Martina below.

"Watch me here," he said.

He rocked up and down, up and down, then launched for the final hold. His fingers touched then latched onto the rock as he rose towards the anchors. His feet cut loose from the rock then his legs swung out from under him as he dangled from the rock. First his left hand failed, and then his right began to peel.

"FALLING," he screamed.

And then he was falling. Ten feet to the bolt, then ten feet more, then farther still while the rope began to stretch and hold and slow him, and finally he was falling no more, he was hanging, in space, between the canyon walls.

He looked for Mina in the canyon but she was gone. The rain was still on both sides, but she was gone.

"What the?" he formed.

"That was a big one," he heard from the rock wall.

He turned and saw her against the rock, ten feet in the air, pulled up to the first bolt he had clipped.

"Are you alright?" she asked.

"Yes. Are you?" he asked.

"Si. What happened?"

"I fell."

Martina rolled her eyes, shook her head, and lowered herself to the ground. Once back down, she lowered Kane to the ground beside her.

"You rest. Then you try again."

"Again? That's a big fall."

"You climb, or you no climb. You decide," she said.

She reached into her pack, pulled out a water bottle and drank. She offered him the bottle. He drank. He shook his hands, his arms. Saw the trickle of water that separated the walls was now more than a trickle. "What's more than a trickle?" he asked himself. "A rivulet? A stream? A freshening flow?" But then the words and the thoughts were gone as he felt her touch.

She took his hands in hers and squeezed. Between the thumb and fingers. Then on the backs, then on the wrists, and then on his forearms. *Mina's touch*, he thought, sinking into her hands, feeling the pressure and the relief and the giving. Then her touch was gone, and his eyes were open, and she was there before him.

"Nice rest," he said. "Thank you."

"Ready?" she asked.

"Si," he answered.

"To the anchors?" she asked.

"But there's no feet."

"There is always feet."

"I'm telling you, there's no feet."

Martina fixed him with her eyes.

Mina's eyes, he thought.

"Kane. Open your mind, then open your eyes. Look for something, anything, a good place to smear. The rubber on your shoes. She sticks to the rock, if you let her. You a doctor. You know science. You know even if they just rest on the wall they take some of the weight from your hands. Open your mind, then open your eyes."

Kane reached behind her again for her chalk bag. Again he intentionally rubbed his hand against her bottom in the chalk bag. Thought for a moment of how she had looked in the ocean, and atop the spire. Felt something change inside him.

"I buy you a chalk bag this afternoon," she said.

"No way," he answered, swishing the chalk bag with his hand inside across her little bottom two more times, as much of a caress as can be had while a hand is separated from skin by a chalk bag.

"Oh," she said. "Kane, you not a good man."

He smiled a flirty smile.

"Kane! You smiled. I write this down. Kane smiled in the rain. You see, I poet too."

"Yes, the rain," he said. "We're going to get soaked walking out of here."

"Maybe we wait until the rain stops. Maybe you chalk your hands again?"

The face on which the flirty smile still resided began to pinken then crimson.

"Climbing," he said.

"Climb on," she answered. "Feet first."

Foot, foot, foot, and hand. Again and again. Until he was at the last move. Where there will still no feet.

"Close your eyes, open your mind, then open your eyes," he heard. Was it from below, or was it from inside. Was she that much inside him now?

He looked for something, anything, a smear. He saw nothing.

He heard it again. "Close your eyes, open your mind, open your eyes."

He closed them. He heard the rain, and thunder. Hard rain.

His hands and forearms began to burn with the lactic acid and blood forced into them from the route, from the overhang, from the effort.

He breathed, thought of waves on the ocean, moonlight on

the waves, Martina's touch on his hand by the moonlit waves.

"Mina's touch, above the waves, limestone soft, on the rock, on my neck."

He said it again, and again, fixing it in his mind, adding it to his words, her poem, their story as his forearms and hands began to burn more and more. There were only seconds left until he would peel away again.

He opened his eyes, and there were still no feet.

"Smear," he said.

He removed his right foot from the secure edge on which it rested. He pasted it six inches higher against the limestone. The rubber held on the gritty friction. He adjusted his right hand. He removed his left foot from the secure edge where it rested. He pasted it another six inches higher against the limestone. It held also. He adjusted his left hand. He raised up on the smears. The pressure in his fingers and hands and arms increased, as did the pain. He took it. Looked at the last hold.

He pasted his right foot another six inches higher. The pressure and pain grew more intense as the rubber held the rock and the angle of his body increased. His hands were screaming for him to just let go, to let it end. But he inched his left foot two more inches higher, then another. His hands were ready to peel, ready to simply fail from the extended contractions. He could even feel his right foot starting to give way on the smear.

"Live or die," he thought.

He reached up for the final hold and it was suddenly right there, in his right hand, then his left. His right foot swung out but his left stayed smeared to the rock. He forced the right back on, then clipped the anchors.

"Mina's eyes...."

"Mina's eyes...."

It was gone, and it had been good.

He sank onto the rope. His chin resting on his chest. His eyes closed. Only the sound of the rain where the words had been.

"Lower," he called.

The cliff face passed in front of him as he approached the ground.

She was beaming, radiant, as flushed with his success on this route as she had been on hers. Perhaps more. Genuinely happy for his success, and to have helped him achieve it. She reached up on tip toes and kissed his cheek. It was salty with sweat.

"BRAVA Kane! You do it! With your style and with your feet!" She stepped on his toe. She reached to hug him, to hold him, to share his success.

He stepped away, closed his eyes, thought, tried to get it back.

"Kane?" she asked. Her arms dropped to her sides.

He remained silent as the thunder crashed once, then again.

"Mina's eyes... Mina's eyes...."

He was mouthing the words. She watched, confused, beginning to feel a hurt. Why had he stepped away? Why wasn't he happy to have climbed such a hard route? In such good style? With her help? With her. Was that it? Was it her help? Her hurt took hold, threatened to grow, maybe to overwhelm.

"Mina's eyes... Mina's eyes...."

Then he had it.

He found a small stick, and scratched it in the sand below the cliff beside the running water. No longer a trickle, now a rush, a foot or two wide and six inches deep.

"Mina's touch, above the waves, limestone soft, on the rock, on my neck."

He exhaled loudly, sucked in what felt like the largest lungful ever, savored it.

"What is it?" she asked.

"It's you," he said. "It's yours."

He pointed to the sand.

She read.

"You did this while you climb?" she asked.

"Si. Did I fall?"

"You no fall, you climb clean."

"Thank you," he said. He stepped towards her, gingerly, tentatively. Reached his arms around her, and held her as gently as he could.

"My pleasure," she said in his ear.

Gentleness and tenderness turned to urgency to intimacy. In the few moments of the embrace he passed from thanking a friend to yearning for a lover. His arms tightened ever so slightly, then the embrace captured his need, his want, his love. He held her and held her as the rain came harder and harder outside the overhang.

"Thank you," he said in her ear.

"My pleasure," she repeated.

The rope was coiled and at their feet as they huddled under the overhanging rock. The rain continued to pour down around them, but they were safe and dry and warm and in each other's arms beneath the rock. They shared tiny pieces of the freshest mozzarella Kane had ever tasted, and figs, and olives.

Kane breathed in to speak.

"No," Martina said. "No more words. Not yet. I still put those words into my heart." She pointed at the scratching in the sand. Where the water had been a foot away, it now began to touch the tops of the letters. To wash them away, grain by grain.

Kane exhaled, relaxed deeper with her in his arms, and closed his eyes.

She closed her eyes and together they slept, beneath the rock, in the rain and in love.

"Kane. Wake up. Kane."

She stood and that pulled him from his sleep.

"What?" he asked.

"The water," she said.

The water was now six feet across, and deeper, and moving quickly.

Lightning flashed and thunder crashed in the gulley. The rain was a solid wall of water.

"We go," Kane said.

They shouldered their packs and quickly moved downstream, towards the shore.

"Quickly," he said.

They moved as fast as they could, as fast as they ever had. Lightning and thunder crashed simultaneously, blinding and deafening them in the canyon.

A freight train sound with tearing and crashing built in the distance behind them. Ahead, the path narrowed and Kane now understood how the tangled trees had come to be in the canyon. Flash floods. In which he and Martina were about to be caught. There was no way back through the tangle they had crossed earlier in the morning. The little tunnel was now underwater, and the tangle was too high, with too much current against it. They stopped, waited, then turned back upstream. The sound of the destruction hurtling down on them grew, shrank, then erupted into shrieks and pounding.

"Up!" she yelled over the noise.

They scrambled up the boulders at the side of the trail.

"Higher," she yelled.

She pulled onto the rock face and moved up and away. Kane reached for the face, but there was nothing to hold. No hands, no feet, nothing. And she was gone. Gone over this blank face. Gone above him, disappearing from sight. He knew she had not fallen, that she was somewhere above. But he was powerless to get there. The screeching and tearing and crashing of destruction seemed almost upon him.

He was alone. Again. Abandoned.

"KANE. Climb the rope!" she yelled.

A knotted rope snaked down the rock above him.

He latched on and pulled with his hands and smeared his feet against the blank face she had scaled. After fifteen feet she was there, on a ledge, beside a cave, with the rope anchored behind her. As he collapsed beside her the full force of the flash flood emerged below them, driving trees and boulders and destruction before it. The dry path on the canyon floor disappeared below the muddy raging torrent.

"Life with you is dangerous."

Imprecision

Her hand rested gently in his. He could feel her pulse, just behind her thumb. It was still very fast. Was it still from the escape? Or was it from the walk back to town along the winding mountain road? Maybe a little from his touch? No, he realized, it couldn't possibly be that. He'd never had that effect on women, not even his very few lovers.

Once again their walk was uninterrupted by pointless talk. He'd never been completely comfortable in a silence, especially when there was someone nearby. He'd always felt the need to fill the void, to remind himself that he was not alone, that he always had the words to keep him company. Yet once again, with her, he remained quiet, and even though only an hour removed from the danger, almost content.

The roofs of the town came into view. Her hand slipped from his. Her pace quickened. Kane started to step out, to try to keep up, but was simply too tired. Why had she pulled away from him the moment the town came into view?

"Martina," he called.

She stopped. Turned.

"You go ahead. I can't keep up."

"Kane," she said. "Are you alright?"

"Yes. Just very tired."

Martina surveyed him. Took his hand back in hers, and began slowly walking towards town.

"I know you're late for your interview," he said. "We should have been back by now. You go ahead. I don't want you to be too late."

"Kane, you a good man," she said.

"So I'll see you later?" he asked.

"Si."

She had pulled ahead a few feet.

"At my rooftop?"

"Si, si," she tossed over her shoulder without looking back. "Later…"

He watched her pull ahead, amazed at the strength and grace of her powerful stride. Even with that Achilles. He could not imagine the trauma of that injury, to a prima ballerina at the peak of her career. He slowed, then stopped. Sat on a low wall that ran along the road now that he was closer to town. Town. Where he had his rooms, and where she had hers. Where their paths were more than crossing, were temporarily merging. Town. Where there were people who knew about her, about him, and now about "them". Town. Where his colleagues from Doctors With Passports would descend shortly for a meeting and where her friends would visit, likely to overlap. Where Fabrizzio waited. Will they meet? Should I plan a dinner? A lunch? Maybe drinks on the rooftop garden at my hotel? Plans, more plans. Kane realized he was doing so much more planning than he had for such a long time.

And then he had an idea. "My friends and hers," he thought. He pictured the doctors and the sponsors, the climbers and the children, the clinic and the climbs. His thought took form, emerged complete. He stood, and slowly walked towards town, towards his new plan.

Plans. For tonight. With Mina. On the roof, in my arms, in my heart. More words. To add to those he'd formed on the climb, and scribbled in the sand. Words. So many new words, and all about Mina.

Vigil

Kane checked his cell phone for the eighth or ninth time. There was still no message. He knew it was working because he had received calls from both the director of the hospital back home and from the local woman who was finishing a painting for him. So why had she neither answered his messages nor called him back. Most importantly, why wasn't she here? Was it the interview? Fabrizzio? The sponsors?

Plans. He'd made plans. Plans for the evening, and beyond. For the first time in such a long time he had made plans. He had purchased two bottles of wine, one white and one red, unsure of which was her favorite. He had five different flavors of gelato slowly melting in a bucket of ice Tetsiana had put beside the table. He had arranged and rearranged the furniture on the rooftop garden until the chairs were just close enough and facing what Kane considered to be the most spectacular of the many spectacular views. Being on his own for the late afternoon he had even purchased a new outfit at the local boutique, the one for locals, not for tourists. The chic Italian woman had made him try on at least a dozen combinations before she deemed him acceptable, "for an American". Apparently the locals made no distinction between Americans and Canadians. Fighting words at home, understandable here.

Evening turned slowly to sunset and then to night. Plans. Whose plans? His, but clearly not hers. He went back over their conversation setting up this evening. He replayed it over and over again and again. He tried to remember all the words to decide which, if any, could have been misunderstood. She had heard him tell her when and where. He had heard her say "si" over her shoulder as she hurried towards the interview, towards Fabrizzio.

Maybe the time had been too vague? How exactly would a Russian living in Argentina by way of Paris and Rome interpret 'later'. The place was not vague. It was clear. "The rooftop patio at my hotel." He knew her lodgings from his trip there. Knew they had no patio of any kind, let alone a rooftop patio. He also knew that she knew that his did have a rooftop patio. She had been there. He had held her hand there. Here. He walked to the corner of the garden closest to the sea, closest to the rising moon. He had held her hand right in this spot.

Plans. So hard to make, so easy to break.

The first chill of the night descended on the rooftop and Kane pulled on his new Italian sweater. He wondered, if she ever showed up would she notice his new outfit? Would she like it? Had he ever cared what he looked like? He thought not. Then he laughed for a moment at what the folks back home at the hospital would say or think if he showed up at the 'emerg', or anywhere come to think of it, in this outfit. He imagined the "Don Johnson" and "Miami Vice" comments he would receive. He imagined the stunned looks when his regular nurse realized he owned something other than frayed jeans and stained flannels and t-shirts.

Kane looked at the bucket of gelato and selected the chocolate chip. Taking the light, almost dainty spoon, he started in slowly. Once again he thought of home. Like his outfit, there was nothing like this Italian ice cream in his northern Canadian home. Lots of ice, and ice cream, but nothing like this. And there was certainly nothing, no-one, like Mina. But there were men like Fabrizzio. Interlopers. Men willing to take another man's woman. Kane stopped himself. He did not know Fabrizzio. Did not know that Fabrizzio was what had happened to Mina. And then he stopped himself even harder. Chastised himself for thinking of her as his. He had promised not to take, not to try to own. And in this moment of weakness on the rooftop he had thought of her as his. So he stopped himself short, cursed the possessiveness, and tried to be a good man.

Gelato in hand, moonlight drifting down over the mountains onto the ocean, Kane thought back over their last few days together. Meeting her at Dorgali, walking back over the mountain to Cala Gognone. Climbing at Cala Luna and Cala Fuili. The swim, where he had been so careless about the tide. Their dinners together, the touch of her hand, the touch of her lips. Wisps of her long blonde hair breezing over her shoulder, and the innocent beautiful shy smile when she would brush those wisps back behind her ear. No idea how beautiful she was in those moments. Their time at the clinic. When she had helped him with the children. He replayed every moment, trying to recall each detail. So much detail in such a little time. A Chinese proverb intruded on his exercise. "Even the weakest ink is stronger than the strongest memory." He reached for the pen in his pocket, but when his hand reached the customary spot, his silky Italian shirt yielded no pocket, and thus no pen.

Kane laughed to himself, stood, and went to retrieve both pen and paper.

Five empty gelato containers lay scattered between two empty wine bottles on the floor of the rooftop patio. Kane's hand continued to scratch words onto the yellow legal pad on the table in front of him.

Plans. He'd had no plans to do this. To write about her, or to write about here. Certainly not to write about her here. But once started, it wouldn't end. Those first few lines from his head had reached the page. And then the gates had swung completely open. Like the flood at Thailandia, the words burst forth and carved a new path like the rocks and trees and boulders. At some point, when his hand had cramped, he'd paused and counted the pages. Forty pages in one night. He'd rubbed his hand, walked about on the patio for a bit, and then returned to pen and paper. Considered how the absence of his muse had set him on a binge of food and wine and guilt of ownership and of writing unlike any he could remember. Forty pages. A month's work back then. He wondered if they were any good, wouldn't let the editor creep in, kept him away, and put pen back to paper.

"Just get it out, get it down, you can fix it later," he said.

"Bon giorno," he heard from behind him. Tetsiana, the lovely, lonely, aloof Italian girl who ran the hotel from dawn until dusk surveyed Kane and the ruins around him.

"Doctore Kane," she said. "You here all night?"

"Si, he answered.

She moved towards the bottles and jars. Began to pick them up.

"No," Kane said. "I'm sorry. I will clean these up."

"No Doctore Kane. You go to your room. Sleep. I clean this."

Kane looked at her and saw the look of genuine concern on her face.

"Grazi," he said.

He stood and moved towards the stairs.

"You get your message?" she asked.

Kane froze.

"Message?" he asked.

"From the lovely dancer Martina?" Tetsiana asked.

"No," Kane said.

"This morning, when I get here. I see there is a message for you. Rosa, you know she work after me, at night, she leave me a note. She say your beautiful dancer woman friend leave a message for you. She go to your room but you no there. So, she leave the note for me."

"When?"

"Prego?"

"When did she leave the message?"

Tetsiana felt the urgency in his voice, felt her heart melt towards him, towards the blossoming hurt she felt and saw.

"Come. We look together." She took his tired hand and guided him down the steps towards the front desk.

Tetsiana reached over the counter at the front desk. She handed Kane a piece of paper taken from the slot for his room. Kane looked at it, handed it back.

"Can you read this for me?" he asked.

"Si," Tetsiana said.

"She says she is sorry she no see you. She thinks you must have gone to the clinic, for an emergency."

Tetsiana stopped.

Kane looked at her, at the note, and back at her. As an emergency room doctor he had read many faces and seen many people who had only told part of the story of their injuries. It had made him an excellent poker player, this ability to read faces. And hers told him that the note was not finished.

"Is there anything else?" he asked.

"Si."

Kane waited.

Tetsiana looked down, looked out the door, out the window. Her angelic face would look anywhere but at Kane.

"Will you tell me?" Kane asked softly.

Tetsiana took a deep breath, looked him square in the eye.

"It will hurt," she said.

Kane nodded. "Prego," he said.

"She says she sorry you no think of her before you go. She says a good man would think of her before he go. A good man would leave a note before he leave her alone."

"Christ," Kane said. He moved quickly to the door and once outside began running up the hill to her rooms.

He arrived in the open courtyard at the ancient Italian home turned boutique hotel where she was staying. He was out of breath from the sprint up the hill.

"Is she here?" he asked the two Italian men sitting under the white Oleander in the morning sun.

They shrugged and mouthed "No Inglesi."

Kane had heard them speak good English. Had conversed with them himself just days before.

"Is she here?" he asked louder. They made more non-committal gestures and mumbles. As they mumbled and equivocated Martina appeared in the courtyard. Her climbing pack was in one hand, a small espresso mug in the other.

She stopped suddenly when she saw him. She surveyed his Italian outfit, his up-all-night eyes, his two-bottles-of-wine face. She turned away, leaned down and kissed the air beside the cheeks of the owners then headed for the street.

"Martina wait," he called to her. "Please wait."

She paused, turned, did not step towards him.

"I am going out. By myself. With no good man with me."

"Mina please. I can explain."

She shifted her climbing bag from left hand to right and began tapping her foot.

"Maybe later," she said and spun on her heel.

"Later when? Let's be precise. I don't want another mistake like last night."

"Precise? You want precise? Okay. I see you later if I decide you are a good man who make one mistake or a bad man who trick me badly."

Kane shrank from the words. Knew he was a good man, a guilt free man, a least in this. Knew he had done nothing wrong except be imprecise. He gathered himself and realized this might be his only chance.

"I was there all night. I waited all night. Ask Tetsiana. She knows."

"Kane I no ask another woman if she with you all night."

"No no no. That's not what I said. Not what I meant. I waited for you all night. Alone. By myself. She knows because she saw me when she left and when she got back. And. I have pages."

"Pages?"

"I wrote."

"You wrote?"

"Yes. All night. About you, and me, and here, and us."

"Us?"

"Si."

"You read these pages to me? When I get back?"

"Yes."

"Then meet me here, right here, at seven tonight."

Martina brushed past him and out the door.

The elderly brothers who owned the rooms where Martina lodged had overheard the entire exchange. They looked at Kane and made unfamiliar gestures that he interpreted as somewhat hostile. Proprietary. Unfriendly.

An anger began to build inside him. His eyes narrowed.

"You two know everything that goes on around here. You find out. You ask Tetsiana and Rosa, and then you tell her. You tell her when she gets back."

They looked at each other and made more unfamiliar and unfriendly gestures. He had no doubt that they would spend all day trying to find a way to discredit him.

Splashes

Morning turned to afternoon as the calm ocean spread out before him. Kane nudged the throttle and the Zodiac picked up speed, carrying him towards the cliff, towards the cave. He wasn't sure why he'd wanted to visit the cave, and he really wasn't sure how he'd convinced himself to rent a boat and go out on the ocean, but somehow here he was, approaching the mouth of the cave. Their cave. Where they'd found the Latin writing, and where Mina had found her project. Where he planned to spend the afternoon thinking about her, and him, and them, and what he would say at seven o'clock that evening when he saw her at her rooms.

The sun was brilliant and hot. The cave was deep in shadow. And cool. As he throttled all the way back, he passed from brilliant day into darkest shadow. His eyes adjusted slowly, very slowly. But adjust they did with just enough morning sun slanting in the entrance. In the afternoons, the cave would be completely dark. And as they regained sight, he could not believe what lay before him. Another Zodiac. Tied off to a horn of rock inside the cave. And Martina, clinging to the rock, ten feet above the water, nearly horizontal, her leg trembling.

He opened his mouth to call her name, but stopped himself, unwilling to break her concentration, even now, with last evening's long wait, this morning's dismissal, and the pending appointment to read the pages. Even now, her passion and grace and beauty captivated him, mesmerized him, held him and lifted him and made him better. Even now, with the agony of the previous night still fresh on his unshaven face, even now.

He let his Zodiac drift towards hers. Tied it off to the same horn of rock. And watched.

She stretched a foot towards one stalactite, then placed it back where it had been before. Stalactites, creatures of limestone caves, dripstones some called them, ever expanding, ever growing, features built from calcium. Features built over eons, would their relationship last so long?

She stretched her foot forwards towards another stalactite, then replaced it where it had been. If she had noticed him, she had made no indication of it. She reached behind her back for her chalk bag, but came up empty. She was wearing no chalk bag but her climbing habits were fixed, the incessant reaching for the chalk, the moving up then down then up then down, probing, assessing, then deciding and moving to the next rest, and so on. Fixed, and flawless.

She moved her feet again. Perhaps it was a trick of the light, or of the shadows, but Kane swore that her leg extended several inches farther than it possibly could have. An incredible, extendable leg... Her foot grasped the stalactite, as her hands moved up and back, towards a crack in the ceiling of the roof. They would not hold. She fell, splashing into the water below. Kane's eyes exploded wide, he took a step towards the edge of his Zodiac, ready to dive in after her, but before he could, she emerged laughing and stroking confidently towards her Zodiac.

She saw him poised on the edge of his boat, ready to dive.

She said nothing.

She pulled herself into her Zodiac, toweled off her long blonde hair, toweled off her sleek wet muscles, removed her shoes, and pulled on a dry pair. She tossed the wet pair into a pile of what must have been 50 or 60 shoes. She looked at Kane but still said nothing.

He too remained silent.

He removed his boat shoes, pulled on his climbing shoes, tied his chalk bag to his shorts, and stepped from the boat to the wall. A small ledge, a high tide ledge, ran along the wall, out towards the sunlight, and back towards the darkness, towards her project. He inched towards the sunlight, away from the Zodiacs.

Martina watched him traverse. Wondered if he had followed her. Wondered if this was when she would see "insistent Kane", or "hurt Kane", or someone else unlikeable, someone able to be discarded, someone wounded and dangerous and over. Someone she would cut on purpose, and send away, and never think about again. She wondered whether this was the end, and whether it wouldn't be better if it ended right here and now. But he had said nothing. He had acknowledged her, had been ready to jump in after her, but upon seeing that she was alright, and going to continue, had simply stepped onto the rock, and away from her project. She had not asked for help, and he had not offered any. She had not shooed him away, so he had not turned his boat out of the cave, and was not going to be chased out. Still, he kept his distance.

She sat in her Zodiac and replayed her project. Surveyed again where her feet would be placed and where her hands would be placed. Imagined where her center of gravity would be, and how it would shift, and how she could move through the crux, through the difficult spot, without falling. Although she admitted that the warm water and the cool air were so refreshing on this calm and sweltering hot day, that the falling was no great matter. Especially with one hundred pairs of sponsor shoes to "test".

Kane traversed farther towards the mouth of the cave. The ledge was wide in spots, narrow in others, and there were many handholds in good locations. The movement was easy, and he relaxed into it. He took positions where he could stretch a leg, then a shoulder. He was playing, and stretching, and doing yoga on the rock, above the water, moving in and out of the sun.

Martina stepped from boat to rock. Kane caught the motion from the corner of his eye. He began to traverse back towards his boat.

She moved a foot up the wall, then another.

Kane inched closer to his boat.

She paused, went up, went down, tested a hold, tested a position.

He arrived at his boat. Sat. Took a drink from a bottle of water. Toweled sweat from his forehead, from his forearms. Tried to watch without watching. Failed. Watched.

She moved higher, arching up and back, away from the edge of the cave, towards its ceiling, where stalactites hung down, mostly dry now, one dripping water that had travelled down from somewhere above. She reached back again, positioned her feet, then once again peeled off and splashed down into the water.

Kane waited until she popped up and started back toward her boat.

He stepped back onto the rock and traversed towards her project. He wanted to know what was hard for her. He knew what was hard for him, but he wanted to know what was hard for her. He arrived at the starting position, could hold himself steady, but could find no way to advance. Could not even identify the holds she was using to move up and back. He traversed back towards his boat.

Kane felt her hand in his chalk bag. Felt her dip one hand, then another. Felt her swish his chalk bag back and forth across his bottom the way he had done to her whenever he'd had the chance. He looked back over his shoulder as he clung to the traverse. Her face was almost against his shoulder, her eyes almost even with his. She rubbed her hands together, spreading and smoothing the chalk, then traversed around him, reaching her left leg around his, pressing her body against his, breathing her breath against the back of his neck, as she passed behind him.

And then she was gone. Past him. Back at her project. She looked up, then back at Kane, then up again.

She moved onto the rock, first one foot, then another.

"Seven o'clock," she said. "Don't be late."

Reading

Kane stood on the exact spot Martina had indicated. He stood there at the exact time she had dictated. He stood there holding the pages from his night on the roof in both his hands. He stood there still feeling the motion of the ocean under his thin rented Zodiac, and still feeling the touch of her hand in his chalk bag.

Martina emerged into the meeting area of her boutique hotel. She stopped ten feet from Kane and looked directly at him. Looked in his eyes, as though deciding whether her next step would be towards him or away from him. Kane implored her with his eyes, tried to draw her towards him, if not forever, then at least for long enough to prove that he was without guilt, to prove that he was a man of his word.

"The old men tell me your story is true," Martina said. "They say you wait for me all night on the rooftop garden."

"Yes, that's what I did," Kane answered.

"They say you drink two bottles of wine and eat five bowls of gelato."

"Yes."

"And you say you wrote?"

"Yes. I wrote."

"About what?"

"About you, about me, about us, about us here."

"About us?"

"Yes."

Martina took the first step towards him. She was still undecided. She knew this was her best chance to dismiss him. And that she must do that soon. Before it was too late.

Kane started to smile and started to walk towards her, but she stopped him with a gesture and with a glance.

"Wait there," she said.

She closed the distance between them, then took the pages from his hands.

"I read, you wait," she said.

Kane had never allowed his pages to be read before. No-one, not even his editors or publishers could see his hand written notes. He would edit and purge and re-write a dozen times before anyone could see. Yet he stood rooted to the spot, obedient to her command, hoping that in this departure from his rules, that he might regain her trust.

Martina retreated into the hotel, and Kane waited.

"Is hard to read," Martina said.

"How so?" Kane answered. His voice was detached. He was about to receive unsolicited criticism on his writing, and from someone who could cut him hard. He'd never sought criticism, and he'd never tolerated it. When he was finished he sent his work to the editor and told them to do whatever they wanted to with it. Criticism was something he'd never endured. He told himself that while he was willing to accept her teaching on the rock, he was not so willing to receive her teaching about his writing.

"Your letters are very close together, and your hand writing is not very clear."

Kane couldn't believe what he'd heard.

"My hand writing is not very clear?" he asked.

"No. And you spell some words wrong. Even I see that. What kind of writer are you?"

"You don't like the way I spell?" he asked.

Martina tried not to laugh, but slowly the corners of her mouth turned up and her cheeks turned red and she could stifle it no longer. She burst out laughing as she crossed the room and handed him back his pages.

He rolled his eyes at the mock criticism. He was expecting character analysis and dialogue critique. But she had said his handwriting was no good. He laughed out loud.

"I love it," she said. "When you finish, can I be the first to see?"

"Yes," Kane answered. "You will be the only one to see."

"No Kane. Is a good story. Some of it even happened! Maybe not just like you write, but sort of. So you show everyone."

She kissed the air beside both his cheeks and took his hand and led him towards a small table in the dining room.

Invasion

Martina's hand lay gently in Kane's.

The remnants of a bottle of wine and a plate of a tiramisu decorated the small table in the corner of the dining room. It was their first meal indoors. So far they had eaten outside. But heavy rain like that which had caused the flash flood had started up again in the afternoon, and then continued throughout the evening. Candles tried but did not completely succeed in chasing the heavy wet oppression from the evening air. Both Kane and Martina were wearing sweaters, even though seated inside.

"Is like this every day in the rainy season," she said.

Kane cast his glance out through the open windows and into the rain soaked night. His mind played back over the flood, and his night on the roof top, their encounter in the cave, and then his day of agony, waiting for her return.

"Hmm," Kane added.

"There are one or two storms like this, and then a few more weeks of beautiful weather, but then it rains like this for what seems like forever."

"Like Indian summer at home."

"Indian summer?"

"At the start of fall, there's always a storm that chases off the heat and humidity of the summer. You know fall is coming, and then winter, always winter. Ice on the cliffs, ice on your car, ice everywhere. But first there are a few weeks, sometimes only ten days, when the leaves have all changed color and the days are crisp and clear. It's the best and worst time of the year. People try to get in that one last "summer thing", because they know the snow will fly soon. There's joy in how clean and clear it all is, and an urgency because it will all soon be over."

Kane thought about the foreshadowing in this rain storm, and about his description of Indian summer. Felt that it was the beginning of an end. He knew what the end would feel like, having felt the emptiness all day when he did not know whether Martina would ever speak to him again. He'd glimpsed the void when Martina had hurried off to her interview and to be with Fabrizzio and he'd stared into the abyss during his night time vigil, only able to avoid its clutches through his work. But today, before her glance in the cave, before he knew whether she would return, and even if she did, whether she would speak to him, he had seen and felt the emptiness. It was so much fresher and sudden than he'd imagined. With his wife, he'd had years to prepare for her passing. And the last day hadn't arrived suddenly, the last day had really been two last months of intense suffering until finally she had crossed over, with the drugs he had left out for her. With Martina the possibility of the loss had been sudden, beyond his control, and irrational. And something about it felt intentional.

"I don't think I'd like it here during the rainy season," Kane said.

"In a way it is sad, but in a way I like it best," Martina said.

"How so?"

"There are fewer people. And almost all of them live here. This is their home. Now, half the people are tourists, and many of the workers are only here for the season. Strangers tending to strangers, with the locals invisible in the background. Is a different place after the tourists go."

Kane considered her analysis. Yes it must be a different place. And yet it must be more essentially itself, more accurate, more genuine. He imagined that the children at the clinic would still need care, perhaps even more so during the cold and rainy season.

"They were very clever," he said.

"Who?" Martina asked.

"The Doctors With Passports people. You know, my friend who is coming in day after tomorrow. They arranged this for me during the best weather here, and during some insufferable weather at home. It's so hard to get doctors to do this, so I guess they stack the deck in their favor. I'll have to ask him about that when he gets here."

"Will he go to the clinic with you?" Martina asked.

"Yes. He'll come to the clinic, and then we're going to do a visit to another area that has made a request for a visiting doctore."

"Do they have another volunteer?" Martina asked.

"I don't know."

"Do you want me to mention the clinic, and their work, in the interview? You know my sponsors may be able to help. They have a real commitment to this area, and to its people."

Kane marveled that they had come up with the same idea. He was certain he had not mentioned it.

"Yes. I think that would be a good idea. But let's ask my mentor when he's here, and then maybe you and he can pitch it to them together because we'll all be at that dinner together in a couple of nights."

Martina shook her head, making a mental note to make sure it got done.

"Will you come back next year?" she asked. She held his hand a little tighter.

"Will you?" he asked.

"With you?" she asked.

They shared a nervous laugh. If Kane had been standing he would have scuffed his foot in the dirt, looked down, and resembled every bit of the junior high boy asking the junior high girl to dance.

"I would come here just to help the children," he said.

Disappointment registered in her face. Not quite shock, but disappointment. And, relief. Had her questioning of Kane's whereabouts last night, and her skepticism of his answer this morning distanced him that far from her so quickly? Would it be that easy, and painless? Hadn't he been a little more aloof than normal over dinner?

"But if I knew you were going to be here, that I would have a chance to see you, I would arrive a month early and I would stay for an extra month," he added. "Just for the chance to see you."

The disappointment vanished, replaced with something approaching hope, something approaching joy.

"So when your mentor is here, you arrange it. And when the sponsors are here, I arrange it with them. For next year. We both come back here. Right here. Next year."

"It's a date," Kane said.

"Si. A date."

Contact

Kane sat in the Internet café that overlooked the harbor. Yesterday's rain had been replaced by today's crisp, fresh air. The clear waters of the Mediterranean glittered in the morning sun. A fresh cappuccino sat to the left of his laptop computer, a small notebook to the right. His fingers moved quickly, expertly, over the keyboard as he continued his messaging exchange with Dr. Bill Federici, his mentor at Doctors With Passports.

"So Bill, you've got everything arranged? Transport from the airport? A room? Everything?"

"Yes Kane. Try to remember who is the organizer and who is the volunteer. Didn't I have everything arranged perfectly for you? I can look after myself."

"Okay, just trying to help," Kane answered.

"So how's it going?" Bill typed.

"Good. The kids are doing great. I've got some ideas for the clinic."

"Ideas? So you might come next year?" Bill asked.

"Yes. You can sign me up when you're here. And I'll stay an extra two weeks, or even a month, if you can arrange it."

"Thanks Kane."

"Say Bill, while you're here, there's someone I'd like you to meet."

"Martina Fuccentesse?" Bill typed.

"How did you know?"

"Dude. I can read. Or at least I can look at the pictures. And I saw your picture together in the New Yorker, the Toronto paper, and even a few tabloids."

"What are you talking about?"

"You don't know?"

"No I don't know."

"Well. Apparently you two cut quite a figure. Climbing cliffs right out of the water, sunbathing au naturel, volunteering together at the free clinic, holding hands in the moonlight. And with your back story and her back story. I guess it's all too much for the papers to ignore."

"Bill. Do respected physicians actually refer to each other as 'dude'?" Kane asked.

"When one of them is hanging out with Martina Fuccentesse,

yes."

"Touche. But Bill. You can't make a big deal about meeting her. She wouldn't like it. And it would make her go all 'public' for the dinner".

"Public?"

"Yes public. It's like she's two different people. One when it's just the two of us, and another when the public is around."

"So she's just like you then?"

"I beg your pardon?"

"So then she's just like you?"

"I heard what you said. What do you mean?"

"I mean that for the twenty years I've known you, you've been at least two people, more like three people. There's Doctor Kane, the emergency room doctor. All clinical and smart and analytical and yet still kind. Especially to kids. Then there's Kane the reluctant famous author. He's still smart, but he's much more emotional, but only when he's writing. When he's in public, like when he's doing a reading, you can tell he's smart and emotional, but you only get a hint of it. You keep it hidden, like you don't want to share, even though you've shared the much more intimate writing. And then there's 'just Kane', or 'jackass Kane' as I prefer to call you. And 'just Kane' is a good guy. Fun, funny, considerate, always on time, and down to earth, especially for a famous gazillionaire writer slash doctor."

"Bill?"

"Yes?"

"You'd better be ready to meet another Kane. Kane with Martina. Kane in love."

"So it's all true?"

"I don't know, because, like I said, I haven't seen it. Anyway, if you can just shake hands and say hi and talk to her like everybody else I'd really appreciate it."

"So no autographs?"

"Dude."

Martina sat in the breakfast room at her boutique hotel. The scent of fresh flowers mixed with her large coffee and the fresh fruit set out on the side board. The breakfast room brought the morning light in from the sky, in from the ocean, and welcomed the guests to wake up slow, to savor the cool crisp morning before the coming heat of the day.

Martina was waiting, again, for Fabrizzio. Why was he always late? Though there were many things she admired about her long time Italian friend and sometime lover, punctuality was not one of them. As she nibbled on a fresh piece of melon, she thought back over all the time she and Fabrizzio had spent together. All the climbs they had done, the days and weeks and hours they had shared. She often thought that Fabrizzio had been the ideal partner. But in reality he, like every other man she'd known, had ultimately disappointed her. While she still looked forward to seeing him, and cherished their friendship, she knew it could never again be more than just a friendship. Not since Kane.

Why was he late? His tardiness gave her a few more minutes to think about him. She realized that his habitual lateness indicated a fundamental lack of respect for her. If he respected her wouldn't he respect her time? How busy she was? Wouldn't he know that she had things to do and people to see and rocks to climb and wouldn't he respect that? How different were Fabrizzio and Kane. Kane was always on time. Always. Early in fact. Not only would he show up on time, but he would leave on time. He was convenient, though at times damned inconvenient. Like now, when she was trying to think about Fabrizzio, and what she was going to tell him, and yet Kane came into her thoughts.

"Bella serra, bellisima", one of the old man from her hotel interrupted. "Signor Fabrizzio is here. Do you want to see him?"

"Si. I'm expecting him," she answered.

The old man winked as he turned towards the hotel foyer to retrieve Fabrizzio. A minute later he showed Fabrizzio into the breakfast room.

Fabrizzio walked directly to Martina, took both her hands in his and kissed the air beside both her cheeks two times. His eyes met hers and held them for a second.

What is this power he has over me? Martina thought. *Why can't I just look away? He's kept me waiting for nearly half an hour and then just waltzes in here without even one word of apology and now I get lost in his eyes?* She forced herself to look away, motioned towards the sideboard.

"There's fresh fruit, and some beautiful prosciutto and

cheese," she said.

"You are very lovely this morning," he answered.

"Why are you late?" she asked.

"Am I late? You said to meet for breakfast. Is still breakfast time no?"

"I said meet at eight. Is almost nine."

"Eight, nine, what difference does it make? I here now, you here now. We eat, we talk, maybe we make love, what difference does it make?"

"The difference that it makes is that I have a hundred things to do before I leave, and I have to get a lot of them done today before the sponsor dinner."

"So we eat quickly, we talk quickly, but the love, not so quickly," Fabrizzio answered. Still no apology.

"I'm done eating. Why don't you get something and then we can talk."

Fabrizzio moved to the side board, picked out his favorites, and returned to the table.

"So, since you are in a hurry, why don't you tell me what you want?" Fabrizzio said.

Martina did a slow burn about his accusation that she was in a hurry. About how he was trying to turn things around on her. How could he always do that? She'd planned to spend an entire hour with him this morning, and now she was only in a hurry because he was so late.

"Fabrizzio, will you consider helping me present an idea to the sponsors?"

"For a climb? For us? Of course," Fabrizzio answered.

"Not for a climb. And not for us," Martina said.

Fabrizzio did not answer. His shoulders made a miniature shrug and his face gave the dismissive Italian look known to all the women who have ever received it from all the Fabrizzios. His dismissive look changed when he saw that she would not give in to his little hurt, would not instantly seek to sooth his affected petulance.

"If not for a climb, and not for us, then for who?"

"Not for who. For what. There is a clinic back in the mountains. They help children. These children have no doctors. So doctors from other places come here to visit. Some doctors are climbers. So my idea is to have the sponsors work with the organization that helps staff the clinic to get more doctors to come here. The climbing doctors and nurses. The children get a doctor and the doctors get to climb in this beautiful place. The sponsors get to help the children and the sponsors could also get some good publicity. I would like our mutual sponsor to help arrange for locals to climb with the doctors. Not all the time, but once in a while. And also to do a bouldering event back in the mountains. There are some interesting boulders right near the clinic."

"Ah yes, I have been back in those mountains. There are many attractions on this island."

"So what do you think? Will you help?"

Fabrizzio did not answer. Instead, he wrapped an impossibly thin slice of prosciutto in an equally impossible slice of provolone and slowly began to eat. As he ate he appeared to consider her idea. While considering, Rosa, the young waitress, approached the table and asked if they wanted more coffee. Fabrizzio's eyes tracked over every inch of her young figure, then stopped when he reached her eyes. As he had with Martina, he seemed to hold her with just his gaze.

Martina witnessed the entire performance. Of course she had seen it before. He was Fabrizzio. He looked at women. That was what he did. That, and climb, and drink coffee, and tell stories. But mostly he looked at women, and women looked at him. They looked at him exactly the way Rosa was looking at him right now.

Martina slowly pushed her chair away from the table. "So, Fabrizzio, like I said, I've got a lot to do today. Maybe you can think about whether you want to help me. For now, I'll leave you two alone." She stood, turned, and left the breakfast room.

"More coffee, yes, of course," Fabrizzio said to Rosa.

Redpoint

"The air is dry, and cool. It will help with the climb," Martina said.

Kane nodded. And listened. Martina had been unusually chatty on the walk to her project. She had walked more slowly than normal, and had talked almost non-stop. Doctor Kane was listening carefully, analyzing, looking for signs of what had brought on this anomaly. Writer Kane was adding a word here and there to his poem about Martina. Kane in love was just happy to be here, with Martina, for what would likely be her last chance this season at her project. This project was the climb for which he had held the rope before, when in his mind she had climbed it, but in her mind she had not.

"Ethics," she said. "Style. Each person has a standard to which they hold themselves. They don't consider a climb, or a poem, or a task done until they have done it to their standard. So today I climb this route to my standard."

Kane continued to listen, to watch, to write, and to love. The combination of doing all these things at once kept at bay the realization that his time with Martina would soon be done. That there would be an acceleration. From this timeless time, to the time of schedules, and mentors, and sponsors. That their time would be less their own the next few days, and then they would both leave. And what would happen then, he wondered. Emails? Letters? A phone call? Would he pester her to meet? Try to attend events at which she would appear? Would she decide to climb near his home? Near his emergency room? Would she turn an ankle and need his care? Just Kane realized that Writer Kane was indulging in fantasy and retrieved Kane in love, bringing him back to the moment. In that moment Kane in love felt, for a brief but painful and poignant time, the gaping loss he knew he would feel when she was gone.

They reached the part of the hike where they had to step around the bulge in the rock to reach the climber's trail. Martina stopped, turned, looked for Kane.

"You remember this part?" she said.

"I remember everything about this part," he answered.

Martina's torrent of words ended. She scrunched down her eyebrows and scrunched up her chin in her own unique quizzical look.

"What you say?" Martina asked.

"I said, I remember when we walked over here, and when we stepped around this boulder, and onto the trail. I remember the color of the ocean, and the smell and feel of the salt mist. I remember the angle of the sun and how it lit up a strand of blonde hair that had come free from your pony tail. I remember how you went up and down and up and down trying different sequences on your project. I remember the joy in your face when you climbed the route, and I remember your explanation of how it wasn't done yet. I remember the touch of your hand on my shoulder, of your lips on my neck, of my body against yours, the warmth, scents, the sounds, the feel. I remember it all."

Martina's expression turned softer. It was the look of a woman who realized how deeply she was loved, and how the love was from a good man. Her soft expression gave way to something else though, as she realized the love was from the wrong man. Why could Fabrizzio never feel or say what Kane could feel and say? Why had she let this older man love her? Kane waited for her expression to turn even farther, to turn to sadness in the realization that it was about to end. But this he did not see. Instead he felt her hand on his shoulder and her lips on his cheeks as she kissed him twice on both sides of his face.

"You are a good man Kane," she said.

Martina was ready. She had stretched and warmed up on an easier route and then stood at the base of her climb for several minutes remembering and reliving and pre-living every move, pantomiming every sequence, climbing the route in her mind before hand or foot ever touched limestone. This was the part of her climbing he loved the most. Though he admired the grace and power and beauty of her actual movement on the rock the same way that he had enjoyed her precision and balance and effortless movement on the dance stage, it was this mental part that he enjoyed the most. After watching her on several routes and several boulder projects, he could tell when she would and would not complete a climb based on the detail and precision of her mental preparation. He knew this would go.

"On belay?" she turned and asked him.

"Belay on," he replied. His eyes scanned her face, her stance, her expression. He already knew that she would climb the route.

Mina's hand touched the rock.
"Mina's hand, on the rock, on my neck."
Mina's feet stepped onto the rock.
She balanced left, reached up, and then was off.
Kane turned his back to the base of the cliff so he could watch her ascend the wildly overhanging route. By the top, the route would be forty feet from the base of the cliff, hanging over the ocean and rocks below.

Step, reach, clip.
Step, step, reach, reach, step, step, clip.
Slowly but surely she ascended. Gone was the looking about, the hesitancy, the probing. She may have been climbing with her eyes closed for all he knew because the movement up the rock matched the dance she had performed on the sand. Step, reach, balance, shift. Step, step, REACH, clip. The only difference between her ascent and her dance was that the ascent moved physically what she had already moved mentally.

Mastery.
That was the word that came to him.
Complete and sheer and pure mastery.
Earned mastery. Not a fluke, not luck, not a dream. Hard-earned mastery. Of her craft and of this route. Mastery of a second realm, of the rock, after the injury had ripped her from her first love, the ballet.

"Watch me here," she called down from near the top. There was a tension in her voice he'd never heard. Tension and joy at the same time, born from the effort of working at her limit. Concern that something earned through so much effort might be lost.

Kane bent his knees, prepared if she fell to jump and make the catch on the rope more soft. But he knew there would be no catch, that she did not need him here on this route, and that she did not need him in her life. Though they were together on this route for this incandescent moment, and though they were together here on this island for these incandescent days and weeks, when the route and the island were gone, their love, his love, would likewise be gone.

Step, step, LUNGE, clip.

She was done.

"Kane. It goes!" she screamed in joy and excitement and surprise. "It goes."

"Alright," Kane yelled up.

"Take," she ordered. Kane took up the slack on the rope and felt some of her weight on the rope.

"Got," he replied.

She leaned back to weight the rope, and at that moment Kane felt the rope go slack in his hand.

"NO," he screamed as he watched her somersault backwards from the top of the cliff. The rope whipped back against the rock and went completely slack in his hands. She plummeted down, accelerating, wind milling and twisting.

"NO," he screamed again as he watched her fall the ninety feet from the anchor to earth. In the split second before her impact he tried to move underneath her, to catch her, to soften the landing. But he could not move quickly enough and then…

And then she was gone. She disappeared from view. Kane stared at the ground beneath the climb. Where had she gone? Where was the body? Had he imagined it all? He looked back up on the rock but did not see her. He saw half a climber's knot in the end of the rope caught in a clip far above. She was gone. Kane walked farther from the cliff and reached the edge of the ledge. There was nothing but rocks and ocean below. Where was Mina?

"She must have fallen out so far she went into the ocean," Kane reasoned to himself. He bent, removed his shoes, whipped off his windbreaker and shirt, retreated towards the base of the cliff farthest from the lip and then raced towards the lip, leaping high into the air and far away from the cliff as he soared out over the ocean trying to clear the rocks below.

Down and down he fell, twisting, and finally plunging deep into the salt water.

He pulled for the surface.

There was no Mina. He dove, then dove again, searching, not finding.

Tears came to his eyes as waves battered him against the rocks.

She was gone. Fallen from her triumph, fallen into the ocean, the ocean that had tried to claim her just days before. Kane dove again and again and again. There was no Mina. He surfaced in a large wave that lifted him and crashed all round him while it gathered him in its power and tossed him towards the boulders on the shore. It threw him high up on the rocks and then retreated to the sea. Kane put his head in his hands. Tears came quickly to his eyes, and he knew that what was inevitable had happened all too soon.

"She goes Kane," he heard.

He froze.

"She goes," he heard again. And then he felt her hand on his shoulder, felt her lips on his cheek. Felt the sun and water and triumph and absurd good fortune of the waves that had thrown them both up on the rocks after her fall and his insane dive from above.

Kane gathered her in his arms. Held her more tightly than he had ever held another person at any time or in any part of his life. Held her more tightly than anyone had ever been held.

"She goes," he said. And then he kissed her, the way a man kisses a woman knowing he has been given a second chance, and that there will be no third.

"You jumped after me," she said quietly.

"Of course," he answered.

"I no believe it."

Numbers

"So now you will tell people about the climb?"
"No."
"No?"
"No. Is just for me and you."
Kane took another bite of his lunch.
Martina locked him with a look.
"And you will tell no-one," she ordered. "About the climb. Or about the fall."
Kane nodded his head in agreement while he chewed.
"How could I tell anyone about the fall? I don't even know what happened! So what happened?" he asked.
"My knot. I forget to finish my knot. I so focused on the climb, I forget the knot."
"You're right. I won't tell anyone about the fall. No-one would believe it."
"I would be embarrassed."
"But about the climb? It's a big number."
"I no chase numbers. I embrace my passions," she said.
Kane nodded again.
"Now, I go and meet Katia."
Martina stood, wrapped her arms around him while he sat, kissed him on the cheek and then spun away towards her rooms, towards her friend.
Kane finished his lunch, taking long looks down the street at her rooms, and even longer looks at the cliffs that rose behind the town. Without realizing it, pen was in hand, paper was beneath pen, and the writing began.

Numbers

No numbers shall I chase,
Though numbers I have owned,
It's passions I'll embrace,
Both novel and well known.

No image shall I chase,
Though many roles I've known,
It's passions I'll embrace,
Outside, and in my home.

No numbers shall I chase,
Though sponsors bitch and moan,
It's passions I'll embrace,
It's stereotypes I've blown.

No limelight shall I chase,
Though cameras I have known,
The passions I embrace,
No photo ever shows.

No numbers shall I chase,
Though dollars surely flow,
It's passions I'll embrace,
For sense and sense alone.

No lover shall I chase,
Though lovers I have known,
The passionate I'll embrace,
Their love shall be my own.

No numbers shall I chase,
Though chase them others do,
It's my passions I'll embrace,
Do you embrace them too?

He signed it…
Martina, this is for you. Though you only said 'I chase no numbers, I embrace my passions', this is what I heard. Love,

Kane.

He walked down the street to her rooms, folded the sheet into an envelope, and left it for Martina, handing it to one of the ancient men in whose hotel she resided.

Analysis

Martina and her oldest and dearest friend Katia walked arm-in-arm along the sandy shore. A brisk breeze off the sea continued to throw large waves against the beach. Martina brushed a stray wisp of hair out of her eyes.

"So what's he like?" Katia asked.

"Kane?"

"Yes Kane. Who else silly?"

"He is a good man."

"Good how?" Katia prodded.

Martina thought. Thought about him waiting for her on the cliffs above Dorgali. Thought about him waiting quietly for her to speak. Thought about him pulling her from the undertow, and thought about him diving into the ocean from the cliff after she had fallen. They walked further along the shore. Her eyes went from the sea to the sky. She heard Kane's words, "Mina's eyes…"

"Good thoughtful. He is a healer, a rescuer. He lives an examined life."

"An examined life? Sounds boring."

"No. Is good. He thinks about how his actions affect others. And he lives so much for others."

"How so?" Katia prodded further.

Martina turned and smiled at her friend.

"Is he so interesting?" Martina asked.

"Yes."

"Why?"

"Because for the first time in a long time you are happy."

"You mean since the accident? You're not going to tell me that it's time I moved on are you?"

"No. Nothing so clichéd. And no I don't mean since the accident. I mean since St. Petersburg. When you and Mikhail were happy before your injury."

"I was happy with Marcello too. Not just with Mikhail."

"But not like you were with Mikhail. When you were dancing and young and in love for the first time. With Marcello you had a good life, and you had the girls, but then you also had Fabrizzio. So it couldn't have been the same. So complete. Here, with Kane, it's like you are that lovely young girl again."

"And is it so complete?" Martina asked.

"Yes."

"No. Is not. Because there is still Fabrizzio," Martina said.

Katia froze. She let go of her friend's arm.

"No. Tell me no," Katia demanded.

"I met with him yesterday morning," Martina said. "And climbed with him before that."

Katia frowned, disappointment consumed her face. She looked at the sand and then out to sea.

"So Kane really means so little to you? Are you that cruel?"

"I just met Kane. I've known Fabrizzio all these years."

"And for all these years he's been wrong for you. Bad for you. Don't you remember what he did to you? How he hurt you? And what you've seen of him? Don't you remember that he kept you from ever being completely with Marcello. And now he will do the same with Kane. Or is Kane just a late summer fling in romantic Sardinia?"

"I know Fabrizzio is not right. That he stops things. But I'm not sure I can ever let go again. Ever let go completely."

"You know he's toxic, and yet you saw him? Climbed with him?"

"Yes."

"But why?"

"For business. Just business. For help with a sponsor. And…"

"And?"

"And maybe for something else. Maybe for a moment. He is the best climbing partner I ever had. He is strong, bold, confident. He needs so little. It was good to see him. Maybe I really saw him for the first time. Maybe because he is here and Kane is here and I see Fabrizzio compared to Kane and I see Fabrizzio for the first time. With Marcello, Fabrizzio was here and Marcello was there, not here. So maybe I never see them side by side."

"How does he compare to Kane?"

Now Martina looked out to sea, the sun in her hair, the mist in her face. Again she heard Kane's words. "Mina's touch, near the waves, on my face."

"Kane is a good man," she started.

Katia waited, knowing there would be more.

"And he loves me. He loves me too much. I don't want him to love me that much. Fabrizzio loves me, but not so much, and not so often. Fabrizzio loves Fabrizzio. And you know how he hurts us. Kane, he will lose himself. I don't know if I can let him do that. Or, maybe I need to let Kane do that, so he will figure it out and go away."

Katia waited, watched her lifetime friend as she continued to look out to sea.

"I suppose it is his choice to make. But I don't know if he sees it. Mikhail loved me, and loves me still, but not like Kane. And Marcello loved me, but still not the way Kane does. Have you read any of his books? I hadn't before I met him. Of course I knew his name. Who hasn't heard of Kane? But now I read his books. They are so extreme. So all or nothing. There's no middle ground."

"And that's bad?" Katia asked.

"Yes. It's too much. No-one can withstand being loved that much."

"What about you? How much do you love him?"

"As much as Mikhail and Marcello and Fabrizzio all put together, and then more, but still not half as much as he loves me."

"Oh my. Does he know?"

"I cannot let him know. It would destroy him."

"Him?" Katia asked.

Martina turned back towards Katia, took her in her arms, kissed one cheek, then the other. She linked her arm in Katia's and slowly restarted their walk down the shore, in the sun, near the waves, with spray and mist all round.

Fabrizzio

"These things are necessary," Martina said.

"Necessary and evil," Kane said.

"Si," Martina said. She straightened his tie, flattened his collar, and kissed the air beside his cheek. "But maybe not so bad this time."

"Why not this time?" Kane asked.

"Because we go together," Martina answered.

Kane took her hand in his.

"Good point," he said.

Kane did not like Fabrizzio. He'd never met him, never talked to him, never even heard about him until a few days before, but he didn't like him. And there he was at the other end of the table. The other end, where the sponsors and reporters had shepherded Mina and now dominated her time. Leaving Kane at the end of the table, under the oleander trees, seated beside the "plus ones" of the sponsors and reporters. One of them knew him, two didn't. The one who knew him had already given him "the look." Kane was thus already into his second glass of wine. A pinot grigio. A fantastic pinot grigio that momentarily made him one percent less jealous of Fabrizzio at the other end of the table and one percent less upset about "the look".

"So there we were. At the base of the climb. The Zodiac had left us and would not return until nearly sundown. It had left me without my pack. So we have no harness, no shoes, no rope." Fabrizzio waited for the dire facts of his latest tale to sink into the sponsors and reporters.

"What did you do?" one reporter asked.

"We are climbers. So we climb."

"With no rope?" one sponsor asked.

"Si. With no rope. With just each other, and the ocean, and the rock."

"What happened?" the reporter asked.

"Well, you know at least how the story ends, because we are both here. But it was a close thing." Fabrizzio launched into the long version of his conquest. The sponsors and reporters hung on his every word. All but the reporter seated next to Kane.

"I've heard it before," she said to Kane.

"I suspect it grows larger with every telling," Kane answered.

The reporter gave a resigned nod and a small laugh. "At least he has one thing that grows larger."

"I beg your pardon?" Kane asked.

The reporter held up her baby finger and wiggled it.

"Very disappointing. But yes, the story grows with every telling. It started out as a nice morning of deep water soloing but now, on its 100th telling or so, has morphed into this multi day epic. Before you know it there will be rip tides, and lightning, and flash floods, and archeological discoveries, and philanthropic medicine, and dramatic headlong plunges from cliffs into ocean waves."

Kane put his glass down on the table.

"I beg your pardon?" Kane asked.

"You've had quite a bit of excitement in just a short time haven't you?" she asked.

Kane refilled his glass, sipped, looked over the rim at the reporter.

"What do you know about it?" he asked.

"I know you're Kane. I know you're climbing with Mina, maybe more. I can see you're jealous of Fabrizzio, who, by the way, is a pompous ass and a dangerous man."

"How do you know about the tide, and the flood?"

"Mina said so in the interview."

"What interview?"

"Oh my. You didn't know?"

"No I didn't know. What interview?"

"The interview she did with Fabrizzio."

"Did you take the interview?"

"No. This is as close as I will get to Fabrizzio. And only in public."

Kane took another sip of his wine. He looked down the table. Saw Mina hanging on each word, just like the sponsors and reporters, saw the admiration in her eyes for Fabrizzio the celebrity. Just then she turned towards him. She smiled her "public Mina" smile at him, then quickly turned back to Fabrizzio.

Kane took another sip of his wine.

"So enough about Fabrizzio," the reporter said. "Did you know that Hemingway stayed in this town after the war?"

Kane tilted his head toward the reporter.

"Hemingway? Now you have my interest."

"Yes. If you go back and read his short stories from right after the war, you can figure out which ones were set right here. I'll bet he even wrote some pages sitting in that chair. Wouldn't you? After a day of fishing? You know he always sat at the end of the table, looking out to sea. I mean of all the sidewalk cafes he could have worked in, wouldn't you think he'd have worked here?"

"Yes. I've written some pages here myself."

Now the reporter put her wine glass down.

"You've written pages here?"

Kane realized what he'd done.

"Are we on or off the record here?" he asked.

"However you want it," she said.

"Off. No on. What the hell. Yes I've written some pages here."

"And?"

"And what?"

"And are they any good? And what are they about? And will there be a new novel by Kane soon? And can I break this story? And is she the reason you've started writing again? It's been like five or ten years hasn't it?"

"I don't know if they're any good. They're different. Not like before. I don't think there will be a novel. Maybe a collection of poems and short stories. Maybe a novel. I have about 50 pages, and in my mind a hundred more. Now that they are in my head, there is only the mechanics to complete."

"The mechanics?"

"The scribbling, or typing. The story is written. You can write whatever you want. About the pages, about me, about here, about her. You're a reporter. You'd do it whether I said so or not wouldn't you?"

Kane took another sip of his wine. Looked down the table where the sponsors and reporters were laughing and following along and egging on Fabrizzio. Mina took another glance down the table towards Kane and saw him talking to the reporter. Her face look puzzled, like for a moment she wondered what they were talking about, but then she looked back to Fabrizzio.

"Why do you say that?" she asked.

"Because in my experience that's what reporters do. Doesn't matter what I say or do, they write whatever they want."

"Okay. Fair enough. How about I meet you tomorrow with my copy and you can approve or disapprove it before I send it to my editor? How's that?"

"I'll be sitting right here at noon," Kane said. He finished his wine, pushed his chair away from the table, turned his back and walked up the street to his rooms.

Morning

"What happened to you," Martina asked.

"I got tired and went to bed," Kane answered.

"I saw you talking to that pretty reporter."

"Please."

"What were you talking about?"

"My writing."

"Really?"

"Yes. She's going to break the story worldwide that I'm writing again. She's going to meet me here at noon so I can approve her copy."

"Kane. I don't know what to say."

"Apparently you knew what to say when Fabrizzio was here, and when the reporters were here."

"Kane?"

"She told me about the interview."

"What interview?"

"The interview you did with the television and the newspaper and the magazine. The interview that was online yesterday, and published today."

"Kane I didn't know."

"Didn't know? Didn't you see the television camera? Didn't you see the microphones?"

"I thought it was just for Fabrizzio, and for the sponsors. I thought they would use it online a year from now, or maybe never. No one cares anymore what I do."

"Is that what Fabrizzio told you? Did he sell it? Did he use you? And no matter what you knew or didn't know, how could you tell them about the undertow and the flood? How could you? Wasn't that just between us?"

Martina took a deep breath. She gently took his hand.

"Kane. I sorry. I very sorry. Please forgive me."

She kissed the back of his hand.

"No-one has ever said they're sorry to me," Kane said.

"I sorry."

"I am sorry too," Kane said.

"What you do?" Martina asked.

"I got jealous of you and Fabrizzio last night. So I just left. I didn't even say good-bye. I'm sorry."

"Did you sleep with that reporter?" Martina asked.

"No. Did you sleep with Fabrizzio?"

"No."

"Why not?"

"Because I love you."

"I love you too," Kane answered.

The reporter approached the table where Kane sat writing. Martina was sipping a mineral water and watching him work.

"It's almost done," Kane said.

"What's almost done?" the reporter asked.

"A poem," Martina answered. "About me."

"Really?" the reporter asked.

"Yes. Maybe you should wait to break your story until tomorrow." Kane held up the long yellow pad on which he wrote. "I wrote this poem about Martina. Basically it's a love poem. I will be debuting it tonight at dinner."

"Maybe I will wait until tonight."

"I can't wait," Martina said.

"You haven't heard it?" the reporter asked.

"No."

"It belongs to Martina. But if it's okay with her, then I want to read these new pages right out loud in front of my friends and her friends and the reporters and sponsors. I want the world to know how much I love her."

"Can I come?" the reporter asked.

"Yes. And bring a camera and recorder," Kane said.

Focus

The beach stretched out, both ahead and behind them. They walked barefoot, on the sand and rock and in the warm water. For miles they had walked, and not spoken. Like the first day, returning from Dorgali. But different. Both comfortable in the silence. Both craving and needing the silence. Refreshing themselves, living, loving, being, being together, and being away from the public lives of yesterday and of later today.

After another mile they came to end of the beach, to the point where the ocean cut inland and separated this part of the coast from the next.

They stood hand in hand on the shore. Tired, revived, together.

"Are those people climbing over there?" Kane asked.

"Si," Martina answered.

"Did they go by boat?"

"You can go by boat. Or you can swim across from here."

"Swim?"

Lifeguard Kane looked into the water, looked for the signs of the tide, of the current. Looked for the beach or rocks or cliff on the other side.

"Si. Swim. I swim across here many times. Is not so hard."

"Do you want to swim across?" Kane asked.

"No. Not today."

"Want to walk back?"

"Not yet," she said. "We have a few more minutes."

Kane looked across the water.

A climber was working his way in fits and starts up an overhanging cliff that rose straight out of the water. Kane looked for, but did not see, a belayer holding the rope below.

"Is that Fabrizzio over there?" he asked.

"Si. I can tell by how he moves. He is so violent. He never becomes one with the rock. His way is to dominate."

Kane considered the tone of her voice. Wondered whether she was describing Fabrizzio on the rock or Fabrizzio in general.

"I don't think he has a rope," Kane said.

"He no use the rope anymore."

"Do you think we should swim over? Offer to hold the rope?" Kane said.

"No. If he wanted me to hold the rope, or wanted you to hold the rope, or wanted anyone to hold the rope, he would ask. He no want me, or you, or anyone to hold the rope. But, he want **everyone** to know he no use the rope…"

"Does he want to die?"

"No. He wants to be alive, in his own way."

She turned her back to Fabrizzio, took Kane's hand, and began walking back towards the town, towards the friends, towards the sponsors and cameras and microphones.

After a mile she stopped.

"Kane. I sorry about yesterday. I lose my focus, just for a minute last night, thinking about Fabrizzio. But only for a minute. I am here with you now. I will not go to Fabrizzio. Never again."

Before

Today at the clinic was going to be different for Kane. The patients would be the same, the maladies the same, the sights, sounds, and smells the same. But it would be different because of Martina. How she had told him that each touch healed him. What she had made him see. How did she keep doing that? Seeing what he didn't see. How could someone like Martina, a performer, be the more astute observer between them?

Kane turned the key and put his tiny rental car in gear. He was surprised, amazed in fact, that the little thing made it up the road and paths to the clinic. The clinic that was becoming more important to him every day. Making him think about visiting more often, staying longer. The clinic with the basalt boulder sitting on the limestone island. Kane thought he was as much of an anomaly there as the boulder. What forces had deposited that boulder there? What had led someone to place the clinic beside it? How had Kane come to be volunteering in the clinic by the boulder? And how had Martina made him see it all so differently?

Today at the clinic was also going to be different for Martina. Kane would still be Kane, and the poor would still be the poor. But she would see each patient as something different. See each healing touch, each kind word, each friendly smile for a scared child as another step forward in time for Kane. As another step out of the solitude he had created for himself. He had so far yet to come. And, she realized, so did she.

It was the little girls he helped. Each one was also a step forward for Martina. A step off that windswept beach, a step away from the explosion and smoke and fire. A step away from the terrible injury in Moscow. A step out of her manufactured world, the protected little world she had created after, and in which she had dwelled these past years.

Tranquility. Peace. Where were they? She now realized they were somewhere outside her new world, and that somehow Kane was on the path between where she was and where she was going. He was on the path with her. Helping her on that path.

But Fabrizzio?

Fabrizzio.

Always Fabrizzio. Even when she was married to Marcello.

He was mean. She knew it. She knew his dark side. Why was he here? There was no way he could help on her path. He could only hurt, and she knew it, and yet she still thought of him.

The cool mountain breeze drifted down off the sharp limestone crags and through the window near where Kane sat and waited for the work day to begin. This was a good time of day for him, before the healing, when the renewal was just ahead.

Then the noises of the day began to intrude. The roosters, and the doves. The gruff voices of the goat herders collecting the flock. But still, in between the noises, the quiet and mountain air were very nearly perfection.

He checked the cabinets and the drawers and their meager supplies once again. He composed a list of items to be acquired, to be produced, to be brought here for the children.

Always the children. With their cuts, and infections, their burns and childhood diseases. And the other.

Always the other. Everywhere around the world, always the other.

From a parent, or sibling, aunt or uncle, a friend of the family. Always the other.

Kane pushed the last drawer shut forcefully, the sound of the wood seating itself echoed in the small room. He calmed himself. Waited for the first patient.

As he waited he mentally traversed the boulder. Remembered the moves he had made, tried to puzzle out the moves he had not. Could she help him? Certainly. Would she help him? He was unsure. Unsure whether he wanted her help. Whether he wanted to keep trying and failing and maybe ultimately do it on his own. Or whether he wanted her to guide him, to maybe make him better than he was? Could he ask her again? As he had that first day above Dorgali? As he had at Thailandia. Before the flood? Or was this something to be done alone? Without her, and her mastery, her perfection, her insights.

"Scusa? Doctore Kane?"

The first patient had arrived. A boy. With his mother, who

was only a child herself.

"Si. Bon giorno."

Mario arrived at her rooms exactly at noon. Which was a miracle of sorts. A miracle attributable to the old men who treated Martina like their daughter and a princess all at once. Attributable to the plausible threats of horrible things that they would cause to happen to Mario if he kept her waiting.

Martina kissed the air beside his cheeks, then stepped back and held out her hand, palm up.

Mario looked at her. Not understanding.

She arched her eyebrow.

Mario handed over his cell phone.

The drive up to the clinic passed quickly, easily, as Mario talked learnedly and enthusiastically about his research, the island, its history.

"People like my professori want the story to be told a certain way. To fit in with how the rest of the world sees us," he said. "But the facts, the truth, do not match their stories."

Martina nodded. Mario was an engaging, intelligent young man when not pouting over his women.

"Match how?" she asked.

"Things developed here much earlier, much differently than the professori on the mainland say. They want Roma to be start and end. To be from where all the islands, including this island, my island, received everything. But the writing you show me. The site I show you. Is too old for their story. There is a different story. A true story."

"Are there other sites? Other evidence?"

"Si. Some I already find. Some I no find yet."

"When will you tell?" she asked.

"Maybe when I think they are ready to hear."

"That may be a long time. Maybe never."

"Si. Maybe never. But I don't need anyone else to know. I only need me to know," his voice trailed off.

"And?" she said, probing, thinking there must be more.

"And I no stand the attacks."

"Attacks?"

"From the professori. From rich men like Fabrizzio from

Rome. They know what they know. They no want the truth unless it is their truth."

"What if I found a site? Or Doctore Kane? He is a very famous man. I am famous too. Would they attack us? Could they attack us?"

"Si. Non. I do not know."

"So what do you do?"

"I go to the cave, almost every day. And I look at the writing, and try to figure what it means. And I look at the pictures, and I look for more in the other caves. One day I go to look in your cave but you and Kane were inside bouldering, so I go to another cave."

"You could have come in."

"Si. And non. But thank you. Grazi."

Lost

Kane cast his professional gaze onto the child before him. He had seen this child before, and had seen bruises like this before. His professional mind remained calm, tending to the physical wound. His personal mind grew more angry by the moment. His eyes drifted to the woman who held the boy's hand. Scanned her arms, her neck, her face. Saw the same bruises, and the same wounds.

"Scusa. Your husband. Did he come with you?" Kane asked her.

"No husband," she said.

"Your boyfriend? Did he bring you?" Kane asked.

"No boyfriend," she said.

Kane shook his head, finished the bandaging, and patted the boy on the head. The boy went to his mother, who stood and left the clinic holding his hand. As they left, Martina and Mario walked in.

"Perfect timing, I just finished," Kane said.

"We go to your boulder?" Martina asked.

"Yes," Kane said.

He took Martina's hand and lead her out, around behind the clinic. A boulder the size of a small house sat on the bare limestone ground behind the clinic. Mario followed a discrete distance behind.

"Is no limestone," Martina said.

"No. It's basalt," Kane answered.

"What it does here?" she asked.

"I have no idea. Maybe Mario knows how it got here. It has no business being here, it's volcanic, and there's no volcano for hundreds of miles."

"Mario. Is there other basalt around here?"

"Non. Nunca. No basalta. I never see this before."

Together they walked around the boulder, inspecting it, looking for interesting features, handholds, footholds.

"Have you climbed on top?" she asked.

"No. I am working on traversing around."

Mario started up a promising line of holds. Martina grabbed him by the waist band and pulled him off.

"Scusa?" he exclaimed.

Martina addressed Kane.

"Do you want to climb up first? Record the first ascent?" she asked.

Mario looked down at his shoes.

"Sure," Kane said. "I'm open to suggestion on exactly how to do that though."

Once again they walked around the boulder together, scanning, studying, evaluating. Finally Martina stopped, pointed to a series of holds, and pantomimed a series of moves that she thought would bring Kane to the top.

"Try here," she said. She handed him her chalk bag and his shoes.

He tied on the shoes and then moved to tie the chalk bag around her waist.

"You will need the chalk. You wear it," she said.

Kane stopped his approach to her, shrugged his shoulders, and tied the chalk bag around himself. Martina walked up to him, reached around behind him, and dipped her hands in his chalk.

"For when I follow you up," she said.

Kane winked, turned, and approached the boulder.

He touched the basalt, its holds seemed laser cut and razor sharp. The rock was very new in geologic time. He stepped up, and, after making the series of moves, stood atop the boulder.

"Brava, a first ascent," Martina applauded from below.

"Come on up," Kane said.

As Martina climbed up, Kane looked around in all directions from the top of the boulder. Below, Mario was talking into his cell phone. When Kane looked towards the interior of the island, he saw the boy with the bruises, and the mother with the bruises, still walking, still holding hands.

"What do you see?" Martina asked.

"A tragedy," Kane answered.

"I don't understand," Martina said.

"That boy. And his mother. Someone is beating them. They have been to the clinic more than once, always with the same types of bruises. I wish I could stop it."

Together they stood atop the boulder and watched the boy and his mother walk hand in hand.

"You do what you can," Martina said.

"Sometimes it's not enough," he answered.

Martina stepped close to Kane, took his hand, brought it to her lips, and kissed it gently.

"You a good man Kane."

While she held his hand, Kane saw the boy and the mother turn off the path and enter a small rock dwelling. A thin strand of smoke rose from the stone smokestack. Two goats and a handful of chickens were penned beside the structure. As he watched, he saw a man approach the front door, look left and right, and then enter the house.

"Time to make a house call," Kane said.

Fifteen minutes later Kane walked up to the open front door. Martina waited with Mario on the path. Kane peered into the darkness, letting his eyes adjust from the evening sun to the dark interior. What he saw appalled but did not surprise him.

"What do you want?" the mother asked him.

"I came to see how you were doing," Kane answered.

"We fine," she answered. She tried to block his view into her home. "You just see us. You know we fine. You go," she said.

"Maria. Vaya!" rumbled from somewhere in the darkness.

Kane thought he recognized the voice.

"Momenta," she answered over her shoulder.

"Is that him?" Kane asked. "The man who did this to you, and your child?"

"You must go," she said.

"No," Kane answered. He stepped towards her, and she stepped aside.

"MARIA!" erupted from the darkness.

Kane's eyes adjusted further, and as they did, the poverty and destruction of her home assaulted his senses. Her boy lay sleeping fitfully on a pallet on the rock floor. A few meager belongings lay scattered about, some broken, some merely worthless.

"MARIA!" this time much louder. The voice approaching.

Fabrizzio stepped from the back room to the front. He stopped for a moment as he saw the figure in the door. He froze when he realized it was Kane.

"What are you doing here?" Fabrizzio demanded.

"What are YOU doing here?" Kane answered.

"Is none of your business," Fabrizzio said.

"When you hurt this woman, and when you hurt that child, you make it my business," Kane answered.

Fabrizzio looked at Maria, then at the boy sleeping on the pallet. He balled his fists, and advanced towards Kane.

"Leave," he said.

"After you," Kane answered. "We go visit the Carabineri together," Kane said.

"No police," Fabrizzio said. "We deal with this here."

Fabrizzio took another step towards Kane, lifted his right hand, and telegraphed a wild swing for Kane's jaw. Kane stepped back easily and let the punch whistle by harmlessly. As Fabrizzio staggered forward after missing with the wild punch, Kane grabbed his shoulder, then threw him down. Fabrizzio rolled across the stone floor, coming to rest against the stone wall. Kane stepped in and kicked him in the ribs.

"Stop!" Martina cried from the doorway. "Kane? What are you doing?"

"What am I doing? I'm teaching him a lesson."

"Stop Kane. I cannot believe you hurt him like this!"

"Me? Hurt him? Look around! Look at the girl! Look what he did to her!"

"What did he do?" Martina asked.

"He's been hurting her, but he's not going to do it anymore," Kane said. "Not after the police are through with him," Kane said.

"No police," Fabrizzio said.

Mario entered the house.

"What is happening?" he asked.

Martina and Kane turned to Mario.

Fabrizzio stood. Rubbed his rib where Kane had kicked him. Then reached into his pocket, and pulled a knife. "No police. No Kane. I kill you here, and bury you in the back."

"In front of all these witnesses? I don't think so."

"You wrong, Doctore Kane. You a weak old man. American. I kill you. No-one will say anything. Not against Fabrizzio. Not here."

Kane stepped backwards, away from Fabrizzio, away from the knife, towards the open door. Martina stepped forwards.

"Give it to me," she demanded. She held out her left hand,

palm up. "Give it to me now," she said.

"Get out of my way," Fabrizzio said.

Martina stood rooted in front of him, staring him down.

"Give it to me," she said.

He raised the knife.

"NOW!" Mario shouted. Everyone in the room turned to him, and saw the .22 caliber pistol in his hand.

Fabrizzio froze. Then slowly, very slowly Fabrizzio walked towards Martina, he tried to catch and hold her eyes. To exert his power over her.

For a moment she was caught in his eyes, but she willed herself not to be drawn in, not this time.

"Now," she said calmly. It was the calm Kane had seen when she climbed, when she moved, when she was focused and in the moment and engaged.

Fabrizzio's hand quivered, then dropped to his side. He dropped the knife on the floor, then kicked it towards the wall.

"Now get out," she demanded.

Fabrizzio dusted himself off, attempted a defiant stare, but like every broken bully before him he only managed a pathetic pantomime of strength.

"So that is how it is Kane? You let this little woman protect you? This little woman and this pathetic boy?"

Fabrizzio spit at the ground in front of Kane then left the home by the front door, and retreated to the path, where he stopped and turned.

"Keep going. Back to town. Now. I will check on this woman, every day if I have to. If there is ever another mark on her or her child, I will ruin you," she said.

"I check too," Mario echoed. "And I go nowhere without this," he said, gesturing with his pistol.

Fabrizzio backed away a few more yards, gestured at the small group in the door of the house, and then stalked away.

Martina walked over to the woman.

"He will never hurt you again," she said.

"Bitch!" the woman screamed.

She slapped Martina, her movement so fast that Martina could not move away in time.

"I love him," the woman said.

The woman looked down, then looked back at Martina.

Slowly she reached up and touched where she had slapped Martina. Her fingers lingered for a moment, and then rose up a few more inches, gently touching the remnants of the bruise on Mina's brow. Where she had hit her head at the beach.

"Oh. Now I see. You love him too."

Revelation

Kane and his mentor from Doctors With Passports were seated at the Cliffside café for lunch.

"So our big dinner is tonight?" he asked.

"Si," Kane answered.

"And I really get to meet her?" he asked.

"Si. Now remember, you promised to treat her just like everyone else."

"I'll try."

"It's easy, all you have to do is set the tone in the first minute. She's perceptive like that. And always reading people like that. If you're genuine, she'll know, and she'll be relaxed around you. If you're not, or if you're fawning, then she'll be Public Mina, and you'll really miss out on getting to know her."

"Sounds like you've thought this all the way through."

"I've thought about it a lot."

"Well, I don't mean to be the bearer of bad news, but do you think she has as well?"

"What do you mean?"

"Do you think she feels the same way?"

"No. She feels differently. No-one could feel like I do, and no-one could feel like she does. We're different. We're all different. You know my theory on that."

"Yes. You've pointed it out several times. And it's an ongoing theme in your novels. But what I'm getting at, is that to the extent that two people love each other at the same time in the same place, does she love you?"

"I don't know. She's a woman. What man ever knows what any woman feels?"

"Good point."

"So. I know you wanted to ask me something about the interview."

"Yes. The interview. She mentioned the clinic, and how her sponsors are going to help out. Did you know that?"

"Yes. We arranged it."

"So you read what she said?"

"No. I've heard it wasn't very complimentary though."

"No. It wasn't. But, thank you for the plug for us, even if you came off a little, I don't know, sub-optimally. Anyway, the visibility will help. And I know a couple of other climbing doctors who, with the proper trip report by Doctore Kane, I might be able to interest."

"You tell me what you want, and I'll give it to you. And, you know I'm coming back here next year. Same time, but for longer right?"

"You tell me when you arrive and depart, I'll make it happen."

"She'll be here too," Kane said.

"At the risk again, of going too far, or making you look too hard, you really need to read the interview."

"The interview, the interview, the fucking interview. No I haven't read the fucking interview and no I don't need to read the fucking interview. You know how I feel about reporters. How do I know she even said half of whatever is in the fucking interview."

"I really think you better read it."

Kane took the newspaper, read.

He folded the paper, handed it back.

"I see what you mean," Kane said.

"Wasn't she somewhat, what is the word, dismissive?"

"Yes."

"Not just of your climbing abilities, but of you as well?"

"Yes."

"That's why I asked if she's in love with you the way you are in love with her."

"I can understand dealing with the press, and minimizing things to protect someone else," Kane said.

"Is that it? Did you see the picture?"

"Yes."

"Aren't they holding hands?"

"Yes. But that's her way. She is quiet, but she likes to hold hands."

"Kane. She's not holding your hand, she's holding his hand."

Decision

"What is he going to do when he sees the picture?" Katia asked.

Martina shook her head slowly from side to side.

"He will understand."

"And will he understand what you said about him? Not just about him climbing but about him? After what you just told me about Fabrizzio?"

"He is in the public eye. He is interviewed. He knows that people protect other people."

"Is that what you were doing? Protecting him?"

"Si."

"It came out a little, maybe, mean?"

"Mean?"

"Yes, mean."

"I was trying to protect him."

"Protect him how?"

"From Fabrizzio. From the people he knows. From the people he does not know."

"I don't get it."

"When they asked me about him, my first thought was to say I love him. That we plan to be together in the future, and that he loves me."

"Martina!"

"That was my first thought. But I couldn't say it. Not right out loud. Not with Fabrizzio and the sponsors and the reporters and everyone right there."

"But isn't that what he's going to do tonight? When he reads his new poem about you?"

Martina hung her head, just for a moment, then lifted her chin and looked straight into her eyes.

"Si. And then tonight, after everyone is gone, I will give myself to him. And then I will make him go away. Or else he will never be safe from Fabrizzio."

"He'll be awfully confused. He won't understand. Someone will show him the interview and he'll be nervous, and sad, and probably hurt. He may not even come to dinner. I think I'd skip dinner if I'd read that about me."

"He will come. He is Kane. He will be on time, and he will

be nice, and maybe he will be hurt. But this is what I was trying to tell you before. He will come and he will love me, he will still love me, maybe even more. And that's why I can't be with him forever, for all the time. Because no matter what I do or say he will love me. And you know I can be cruel. I don't mean too."

"You're Russian, and Argentinean, you can't help it."

"Yes, I can."

Substitution

Martina and Kane stood in the foyer of his hotel, just across the street from where the finale dinner announcing the collaboration between the climbing company sponsor and Doctors With Passports was about to be held.

Martina stopped, took Kane's hand, and looked into his eyes with an intensity he had never seen.

"Tonight we must pretend. Tonight I have to pretend with Fabrizzio that nothing happened, and you have to pretend that I mean very little to you," Martina said.

"How can I pretend that? And how can you pretend?" Kane asked. "After what we saw, after what he did?"

"We have to. I have to," Martina said.

"Why?"

"Because Fabrizzio is a dangerous man. You know that a little. But you don't know it all. And never more dangerous than tonight. So tonight I pretend that nothing happened, and then it will be over. He will know that so long as he does nothing to hurt that woman, that I will not hurt him."

"Why do you care about him so much?" Kane answered.

"I care nothing for him. I care only for the mother, and her child. I protect them, from Fabrizzio, and from everyone. Is different here Kane. Is an island, an old island, with old ways. When you talk about the police, Fabrizzio just laughs. They would do nothing. You think the police would take the side of a poor hill girl against Fabrizzio? Never. You think they would listen to you? To me? No. We are not from here. So please help me tonight, help me help the mother, and her child. Help me pretend."

"I don't understand, but I will do what you say," Kane said.

"Help me tonight, and then tomorrow we go to the girl, we offer her a new life somewhere far away, where Fabrizzio will never find her."

"Will she go?" Kane asked.

"No. I do no think so. But then we know we do everything we can," she said.

"Alright," Kane said.

"Grazi," Martina said. She kissed him twice on each cheek.

A small crowd had gathered in the courtyard overlooking the ocean. Pre-dinner drinks had been served, appetizers consumed. While the majority of the crowd had once again gravitated to Fabrizzio and Martina, the reporter had stayed close to Kane.

"It looks like you're wasting your time over here with me," Kane said.

"Nope."

"All the action is down there with mister congeniality," Kane said.

"I'm not writing a story about him," she said. "I'm writing a story about you, and your writing, and the new poem you are debuting tonight. You're still debuting the poem right?"

"I don't know," Kane said.

"So I guess you saw the interview," she said.

"And the picture."

The reporter tilted her head towards where Fabrizzio stood with his arm around Martina. "And that," the reporter said. A photographer posed Martina and Fabrizzio for a picture with the sponsor.

Martina finished her "Public Mina" smile for the camera, and made her way over to Kane.

"Are you having fun?" she asked.

"Not really," he answered.

"It looks like you are having fun," she said. She tilted her head towards the reporter.

"Nope. Just talking. And pretending. Like you wanted me to."

"Hmm. Looks like more than talking. And it is convincing pretending."

"Speaking about looking like more than talking... Does Fabrizzio have to keep his arm around you at all times?"

"He is Italian."

"And you used to be his girlfriend, and climbing partner. No, wait, his 'favorite, most daring' climbing partner."

"Ah yes. From the interview? I wondered if you would use that against me."

"Yes. From the interview. And the picture from the interview looks like what I am seeing tonight."

"I too am pretending."

"But the picture and the story were from before 'pretending.'

What were you doing then?"

"Forget him. Ignore him. I try to."

"No you don't. It looks like you like it. Don't you realize how that makes me look? Even if you are pretending."

"Ah. So now we have it. You care about how you look. You no care for me, or the girl, or her child. Your man pride is hurt. But why you care how you look? You know the truth. You know the papers and the television mean nothing. You know who is holding me, and kissing me. You know who I love for real. This is all just pretend."

"Pretending. Yes I understand the papers and television mean nothing. But I don't understand about the picture. He was holding your hand."

"That is Fabrizzio, he always takes my hand."

"You could take it back," Kane said.

"That would hurt him," Mina said.

"No. You're right. I suppose you prefer to hurt me instead."

"You wrong. You choose to be hurt. Is different." And then Martina kissed him, on both cheeks, then on the lips. "You get to choose if I hurt you," she said. And then, after another warm, lingering kiss, she left him and returned to the sponsors, and to Fabrizzio.

"What was all that about?" the reporter asked.

"You don't want to know," Kane said. "Trust me."

"Thanks again for agreeing to the interview," the reporter said.

"Part of me wishes I hadn't agreed," Kane said.

"If you don't want me to write it, I won't," she said.

Kane looked away from the crowd gathered around Fabrizzio and Martina. He looked at the reporter and for the first time noticed her eyes. Noticed that she was very young, and very pretty. Noticed that her skin was tanned and that her hair was dark brown with traces of red. Noticed that she had a very pleasing figure.

"No. I want you to," he said. He swept his hand around the patio. "No matter how this turns out."

"Why? Why now? Why after all this time?"

"Because I'm tired of living a lie," he said.

"A lie?" she prodded.

Kane noticed that while Martina waited in conversation, that this pretty young thing was more aggressive.

"Yes. A lie."

"A lie about what?"

"You are impatient aren't you?" Kane asked.

"No. But I am nervous. About meeting you. About being here. About being around all these rich and famous people. I'm just nervous. I'm sorry," she said.

"So. Are you open to suggestion?" Kane asked.

"Depends on what you're going to suggest," she said. She brushed her hand against his, for just a second.

Against his will, he stirred. And for a moment he could feel her young skin, feel her beneath him, could feel himself taking her and ending all this pain with Martina.

"I'm not suggesting *that*," he said, regaining control.

"I am," she said. She held his eyes until he looked away. He took a deep breath and looked back to the pretty young reporter. He noticed that fine mix of wine and youth and exotic places in her eyes. He refused the thoughts this time.

"What I'm suggesting is that when a writer is nervous, especially a reporter, that the writer should talk less and listen more. Maybe compose in their mind while listening. What I'm suggesting is that a writer needs to focus on telling the story, not being the story."

The reporter took a half step away from Kane.

Kane went on. "There's a lot of stories here, a lot of material. If the writer observes, there's enough material for five articles, or even a short story."

"Is that how it always is for you," she asked.

"How what is?"

"Is it always an observation? Are you just a chronicler, or do you ever live on your own?"

"I beg your pardon?" Kane asked, his voice registered his astonishment at the impertinence of the question.

"Other writers have told me that they wished they had written less and actually lived more."

"I've lived plenty."

The reported nodded towards Martina and Fabrizzio. "But like him? And her? And them?" she asked.

"No. Not like them. Though I suppose in this last week or

two I have lived a little like them."

"How so?" she asked.

"Now you're getting it," Kane said. "Let the subject tell the story. There's a story you came here tonight to write, a story you want to write, but if you listen, and watch, and let the subjects tell the story, you get to create something real, and pure, and unburdened with any preconceptions."

The reporter inhaled to ask a question.

Kane held up his hand.

"Don't ask, just let me tell you."

She exhaled and waited.

"It's the preconceptions that frustrate you, that ruin a story. You know how you want it to go, how you want it to end, and you try to force it that way. Consciously, or unconsciously. The subjects, real or imagined, are going to go where they want to go. You're better off just observing them. Now here's what you probably wanted to hear. That's my process. That's what I try to do. In my writing, with the characters I imagine, and in my private life, with the characters I encounter. I try to observe and accurately report. Yes I'll get them into interesting situations in interesting places with interesting people, but then I try to leave them be. If they want to speak to me, to become part of my story, in my writing or in my life, then they will, otherwise they won't."

"So you're indifferent, or perhaps, ambivalent, towards them?" she asked.

"Not exactly either. More like, detached."

The reporter nodded again to Martina.

"But with her, you have been attached, literally, by the rope. And, given the evil look she's been giving me all night, in another way too."

Kane looked away from the reporter and over at Martina. Though Fabrizzio's arm was still around her, her attention had shifted to Kane and the reporter. He saw the "evil" look the reporter described. It was a look he had not seen on her face before.

The reporter continued. "And now, tonight, when you both know you are going to tell the world how much you love her, when you are going to read in public for the first time in nearly twenty years because you are in love, she is with Fabrizzio and you are with me."

"She's not 'with' Fabrizzio," Kane said. "And I'm not 'with' you."

"You could be," she said. "That offer remains open." She looked into his eyes and parted her lips, licking her bottom lip.

"Excuse me," Kane answered. He moved slowly but purposefully across the patio towards Martina. In a minute he was in front of her. Fabrizzio glanced at him, smiled at him, then returned to his audience and his story. His arm remained around Martina. She made no move to escape it.

Kane leaned in close to her, whispered in her ear. "I need to tell you something," he said.

"Not now," she answered.

She swept her eyes around the group gathered in front of her and Fabrizzio.

"Can we talk?" he whispered.

"After a while," she answered.

"It's about the poem, there's something I need to tell you," he said.

"Am I interrupting?" Fabrizzio asked. He looked from Kane to Martina and back to Kane.

"Yes," Kane said.

"Si?" Fabrizzio asked, his voice low and dangerous.

"Si. When you are done, I think these people would like to hear about the clinic, and the help these very generous men and women are pledging to give to the clinic. And while I'm sure these tales of glorious climbing days of yore are fascinating, perhaps these people would like to hear about the future, particularly the future of the clinic, and all the **children** we treat there."

Fabrizzio did not pause, though the threat registered in his eyes.

"Days of yore? Is days gone by si?"

"Si."

"But Doctore Kane, I am telling them about our most recent climb, from this week."

"This week?" Kane asked.

"Yes. While you were at the clinic, Martina and I were together, we spent a beautiful day climbing. Listen, is a good story. I think you have much to learn."

Fabrizzio returned to his audience, returned to his story. Kane listened for as long as he could, but with each word he stepped father away, inevitably returning to the far end of the patio, where the young reporter greeted him with another glass of wine.

"Ouch," she said.

"See what I mean about just watching. You get much better material."

"I see what you mean about interesting people and not being able to control them."

"Did you know?" he asked.

"Know what?"

"That they had gone climbing this week, while I was at the clinic?"

"Yes."

"What else can you tell me about them, about him?"

"Everything. Too much."

"Everything?"

The reporter held out her arm and turned the bottom towards him, the bruise on her forearm angry and distinct.

"Everything."

The dinner was winding down. Martina had come to sit with Kane for twenty tense minutes. There had been only a few words between them, but mostly silence. If it was pretending, it was very convincing. A silence, but not a comfortable silence like the others they had shared. Though he tried, he could not ignore that she had gone climbing with Fabrizzio and not told him. Taken together with the interview she had given, and with the intimate details shared in the interview, he had started to doubt her. He doubted nothing about their moments and days together, doubted nothing about the words and touches they had shared. Doubted nothing about the strength and resolve she had shown protecting the mother and child. But he doubted how well he really knew her, and if she really loved him. But more than he had started to doubt her, he had started to doubt his judgment. And doubted that he had seen all of her. That much was clear. There was this whole part of her about which he knew absolutely nothing. And yet she seemed to be so completely with him when she was with him.

"They are about to introduce you," she said.

"Si," he answered.

"There's something I need to tell you," he said.

"After," she answered. She kissed him once on each cheek, then once on the lips, then walked to sit beside the master of ceremonies.

The host and master of ceremonies for the dinner was the president of the sponsor company. He was a polished Italian man, completely at home here amongst the celebrities and the food and wine and seaside beauty. He had progressed the evening from the wine and appetizers through the dinner and presentation about the clinic. The announcement of the partnership between the sponsor and Doctors With Passports had gone perfectly. Now all that remained was Kane's reading.

"And now, a man who needs no introduction to this group. Kane is the man, the doctor, who you know as the visionary who conceived the idea of the partnership between my little company and the ideals of the Doctors With Passports and the clinic in the hills. Kane is the man who you know as the man who inspired these great climbers to agree to promote the sponsorship by agreeing to guide, along with our local guides, the doctors who visit and staff the clinic. Many of you, but not all of you know that Kane is also a famous man, an author. While he chooses to live a quiet life of service, he also chooses to educate and entertain and move us with his writing. Not so much now, but when he wrote, he moved us. I myself own more than ten of Kane's novels, though until just yesterday I did not know that Doctore Kane was also novelist Kane. More than one hundred million people have read Kane's stories. I will not embarrass him by outing his nom de plume. Instead I will accept the honor he is about to bestow on us with his reading. This is the first, and I understand will be the only, public performance of this piece. So, please join me in showing our appreciation for this unique experience."

Kane stood, nodded towards the host, and smiled a short pained smile. He pulled a folded sheet from his shirt pocket, straightened it, surveyed the table, and then refolded it. He cleared his throat, looked around the table, and then looked down. When he looked up his eyes found Martina's. She was questioning him, sensing that something was wrong. He looked away and then found Fabrizzio. Fabrizzio was staring at Kane, and while his mouth was smiling and his tone was gay, his eyes were dark and dangerous.

Nervous glances began to dart around the table. Kane inhaled deeply, sighed, and then pulled a set of folded sheets from his jacket pocket. He straightened them, surveyed the table, cleared his throat, and began to read.

"This is called the legend of Mina's Leg. If you've ever seen her climb, you may even have seen it."

An incredible, extendible leg,
Supports a woman I know.
It's an awesome sight
Can give you a fright,
To see the amazing thing grow.

Martina almost gasped. These were not the words she had heard him writing, rehearsing, rewriting, mumbling over the past few days. These were not the words he had scribbled in the sand. This was not a poem about love. This was a poem about her leg?

When it first appeared,
In the limestone cave,
I gawked, I stared,
I blinked amazed.

I couldn't account,
But her impish grin,
Left no doubt,
That the woman who'd been,
But five foot one,
Not a second before,
Had for a moment,
Become six foot four.

Fabrizzio laughed out loud. "Si, is true," he said. The crowd laughed along with Fabrizzio. Martina was stunned. Though this was about her, this was not "her" poem. These were not her words. She could not understand what Kane was doing. Where was his declaration of love? Had she gone too far? Had she hurt him too much too soon? Martina searched him with her eyes, but he would not return her stare.

No sound did it make,
As it telescoped out,
'til her foot reached a flake,
five feet, no doubt,
from the climber who perched,
on a rock face so bare,
no hard man would touch it,
not even when dared.
Rock over she did,
On the limb stretched so wide.
Then floated on up,
On her miracle ride.

Returning to earth,
Round the back of the boulder,
She skipped back and forth,
Flipped her hair past her shoulder.

How? I asked,
Through only my eyes.
She kissed my cheek,
Then to my surprise,
Handed her chalk bag
And pointed back yonder.

To the blank polished face?
I was toast, a goner.

Scratching and scrabbling
(up an aluminum ladder)
I later arrived
At the stance where my bladder,
Threatened to empty,
No holds to be found,
Clinging to nothing,
Twelve feet from the ground.

Reach though I made,
With my much longer frame,
My foot never neared,
What her foot had claimed.
Try after try,
From this frustrating spot
Not one inch beyond,
This location I got.

How had she done it?
With that tiny appendage.
When my reach much longer?
Having much greater leverage
could not even touch,
what she had transcended.

Exhausted I lay
With my back to the stone.
I stared at her leg,
Was it rubber or bone?

Will you show me again?
I asked from the shade.
For my insecurity,
A dark plan had made.

Catch her I would
In my digital camera.
Proof I would have,
Of her abra-ca-dabra.

A bad choice to make
To compromise trust
To trample this gift,
In the cold Italian dust.

Kane paused. He looked round the table, making a point with his pause. After surveying all the guests, he caught, then held Martina's eyes. "Compromise trust", she heard ringing in her ears. Yes. That is what she had done. With the interview, and with Fabrizzio. She knew it, and now knew that she was paying the price.

Kane cleared his throat and continued with his story.

She stretched a slim hip,
Then chalked up her fingers.
Looked to the west,
Where the setting sun lingered.

"It's getting late, and the darkness is close.
But one last last try,
Ne fait pas rien chose."

So once more she climbed.
I grabbed my Minolta,
She got to the spot,
Moved not one iota.
Balanced, she waited.
A decision she made.
"Trust him I will,
Though my risk is grave".

Out went her leg,
Growing step by step.
Out past a Hueco,
Out past an arête.
The leg kept on sprouting,
Beyond comprehension,
And then re-appeared,
From the other direction!

My finger never twitched,
No image was captured,
Disbelief filled the space,
In her moment of rapture.

A sprite she must be,
To cast such a spell,
The camera I dropped,
My legs ran like hell.

'Til my heaving lungs,
More breath could not take,
Sense of this moment,
My mind would not make.

No drugs had I taken,
No beer had I drank,
No mushrooms, no peyote.
No handling of snakes.

Senses I had,
Though baffled they'd been,
I rose, turned about,
Returned to the scene.

Where did you go?
She asked from the sand.
Her tone disappointment
In the run away man.

She'd taken the chance
To show me the magic
Risking what happened
Obsession and panic.

I sat down beside her,
Took her leg in my hands.
Pushed, pulled and prodded,
On her gam, firm and tanned.

How do you do it?
I asked right out loud.
My hands kept on probing.
Her leg was quite sound.

"I can tell you," she said,
"but you won't be the same."
"I can tell you," she said,
"if your fears you can tame."
"I can tell you," she said,

*"though no man has withstood,
the full truth of knowing,
my sublime womanhood."*

*As I sat there beside her,
With her hand in my own.
The peace was complete,
More complete than I'd known.*

*"I'll risk it," I said.
"I won't run away."
Share your secret with me,
Be the yin to my yang.*

*So she spun out her story,
Beginning to end,
How her gramma's hot feet,
Allowed space/time to bend.*

*A gift she passed on,
To her tiny granddaughter,
The day that she learned,
She lost her grandfather.*

*More days we spent climbing,
More moments together,
Alone in land,
We climbers treasured.*

*'Til home we both went,
to our families and lives,
consumed though I was,
with the dream so alive.*

*She's out climbing somewhere,
This woman I know,
The sun in her hair,
Her face all aglow.*

With effort and grace,

And style and strength.
With feelings run deep,
With gifts heaven sent.

Her reach still exceeds,
What this man can't know,
And that lithe little limb,
Somewhere it still grows.

Owned she can't be,
But treasured she can,
If you'll listen, believe,
Duplicity ban.

An incredible, extendible leg,
Belongs to a woman I know.

Gentle applause rose from the crowd. Fabrizzio laughed out loud again, but this time the laugh died a solitary death, no-one paid attention. Instead, their eyes were riveted on Martina. She had expected something else, that was obvious. They had all been expecting something else, an overt declaration of love, a moment.

"How could you?" she whispered.

"I can explain," he answered.

"Tomorrow, at breakfast, you tell me why," she said.

She stood, nodded to the table, and ran down the street to her rooms.

Breakfast

Breakfast foods sat untouched in front of each of Kane and Martina. Though their eyes had met briefly while they ordered, they had not engaged. Kane kept looking out over the ocean, Martina kept looking into the hills. She breathed deeply, sighed, then began.

"I did not know you had two poems," she said.

I did not know you had two lives," he answered sharply.

"Two lives?" she asked.

"Your life with me, and your life with Fabrizzio," he answered.

"Is that what it was? You were jealous? So you chose to embarrass me?"

"Me? Embarrass you? Now whose 'man-pride' is wounded? What were you doing with him all night?"

"You know what I was doing. I was pretending. I was protecting them."

"Protecting them? Or protecting him?"

"Stop. Stop. Please stop. This take us nowhere," she said.

She took his hand. It was stiff and cold in hers.

"You're right. It gets us nowhere."

"So. Where are we?" she asked.

"We are here," he answered.

"Si. Here. But where is here? This is not how I thought this morning would be. I thought last night you tell the world you love me. And then I show the world I love you. And, I show you how much I love you. I give myself to you. We be together, as one."

Kane's hand softened, and warmed.

"Together?" he asked.

"Si. As a man and woman. And then, then, you tell the funny story. Not the love story. I no understand."

"But you do understand," he answered.

"A little. But not all of it," she said.

"Even after reading the interview, and seeing the photo, and even after finding out that you went climbing with Fabrizzio, I still wanted to read the poem. To be with you. But whether you pretending or not, you put Fabrizzio in between us. So I couldn't."

"Why not?"

"Because, it wasn't right. It wasn't the right time, the right people, the right feeling. It is done, and I think it is the best thing I have ever done. And I couldn't give it away under those circumstances."

"I no understand."

"It is too personal. Too much just for you and me. I think we are different that way. I think you can love out loud, love in public, and never doubt your lover, or your love. But I don't think I can. I think I am more private, and I know I am jealous."

"Jealous of Fabrizzio?"

"Yes. But not just Fabrizzio. Jealous of all of it. Of how easily you move in public. Of how comfortable you are with all of it. Of how easily you could give me up."

She pinched her lips, nodded her head, brushed her fingers against the back of his hand. So he knew that she would easily let him go.

"And yet. I wanted to protect you."

"Protect me?"

"Si. From Fabrizzio, and from all of them."

"Protect how?" she asked.

"I'm not sure. But I knew, just before I started to read, that to read Mina's eyes would hurt you, would hurt me, would hurt us somehow. And I knew for certain he would not abide the telling. That he would break, and attack. So I read the funny story."

"I liked the funny story."

"You did?"

"Yes. It was very funny. Not what I expected, but still, it was funny. And a love story too, in its own way."

Their hands relaxed the tiniest amount in each other's hands. Their gazes caught and held for a fragile moment. Their frowns diminished in the brilliant morning sunlight that danced off the warm ocean waves.

"I can read it for you now," he said. Kane reached into his shirt pocket and pulled out the still folded sheets.

"Not yet," she said.

"Not yet?"

"No. Not yet. Is not right. Is too soon after the funny poem."

"Then when?" he asked.

"You will know when. And I will know when. And if that

time ever comes, then we will both know that it is our time to be together."

The dishes had been cleaned away, the sun had risen a little higher in the sky. The morning mist had risen from the harbor and yet Kane and Martina still sat hand in hand at the small table beneath the white Oleander.
"What you do today?" she asked.
"I have no plans," Kane said.
"Will you come with me to the cave?" she asked.
"The cave?"
"Yes. In the ocean. With the Latin words. I think I work this project today."
"Yes. Of course."

Kane held the nose of the Zodiac against the smooth limestone wall inside the cave. Martina professionally wielded a yellow power drill that was nearly half her size. While Kane held the Zodiac steady, she drilled then expertly placed a bolt in the hole.
"I always wondered how the bolts got there," Kane said.
"Now there is one less mystery in your world," she said.
"Yes. But compared to the great mystery in my life right now, it is trivial."
"The great mystery?" she asked.
"Yes. The great mystery."
"Which is?" she asked.
"You. Us. Tomorrow. And then…"
She laid the drill in the bottom of the boat. Sat. Looked down and considered, then looked up and caught and held his eyes.
"This bolt I just place. It will be here for many years. The salt and the water and the air will make it rust. But it will be here for many years. It will be here next year. For me to climb, and, if my prayers are answered, you will be here with me."
"You are still coming?" Kane asked.
"Yes, and you are too," Martina said. "You promised the doctore, you promised the children, you promised me."
"Will we be here together? Or will we simply be here at the same time?" Kane asked.
"After yesterday, and last night, and the poem, and

everything? How can you ask me such a thing? You hurt me like that, and now, here, you ask me such a thing?"

Martina pulled on her climbing shoes. She moved all the way to the end of the Zodiac.

"I try the first moves," she said. "You move the boat away. If I fall I go in the water."

She reached up and grabbed the first large hold.

Kane moved the rubber boat away from the rock, away from his love. He looked into the water, considered the waves, which were small, and the tide, which was slack. He moved the Zodiac 'upstream' of where she clung to the underside of the limestone cave.

She moved up a foot, then another.

She moved back down, nearly touching the water.

She moved up the same foot, then turned to Kane.

"Is hard," she said. She motioned with her foot for Kane to bring the Zodiac underneath her.

"This project we will work together. You and me. No-one else. I tell no-one is here, you tell no-one is here. This will be ours. I never tell anyone about it. I promise."

"Agreed," he said.

"Now we go back," she said. "I have sponsor commitments for the rest of today and for tonight. And I know you have many things for tonight. So? Tomorrow?"

Though he knew they were both scheduled and could not see each other, he still felt dismissed somehow. Dismissed by all the people who had descended upon his momentary Shangri La. It made him feel diminished, small. Still, he was willing to take what he could get.

"Yes, tomorrow. Will you have dinner with me? Tomorrow? On my rooftop balcony? Just you and me? No sponsors, no friends, just us?"

"Si."

"So just to be clear, we're having dinner on my rooftop balcony, at my hotel, at 9 o'clock, tomorrow night," Kane said.

"Si.

"Say it back to me. Let me hear you say it. I need to know you'll be there."

"Your hotel, the rooftop, tomorrow at nine, just you and me. But wait, there's more," she said.

"More?"

"Yes. We have another date."

"We do?"

"Yes. Here, this island, next year, this time, you and me. If not for us, then for those children in the clinic."

"Si."

"But it would be nice if it was for us too."

The Cave

The morning fog was thick on the harbor as Kane walked down the quay towards the Zodiac he had arranged with Tesio. It was the morning of their rooftop date. A day filled with commitments and people and things that were not Martina. But before any of that, Kane was headed to the cave. To leave a message for Martina. That she would get the next time she went to the cave.

"Kane? What you do here?" he heard.

"Martina? What are you doing here?" he answered.

"I go to cave, to work the project before I leave."

"I was going to the cave to leave you a note, and a little present."

"Kane you so sweet. We go together. Before our date tonight."

She winked and wiggled a hip.

Kane's heart leapt, along with another piece of his anatomy.

"Okay," he managed.

Kane slowed the Zodiac a dozen yards from the entrance to the cave. The seas were running a little higher, and the tide was running in, so it would be a trick to time up a wave just right to surf them into the cave.

"Are you sure you want me to try this?" he asked.

"Si. We try once. If it no go, it no go and we go back."

"Okay. It ought to be okay if we can time it. Hang on."

He turned his eyes away from Martina and tried to feel the waves, to feel the sea, to feel. After a few minutes, he had detected the pattern of the sets, timed up a wave, and easily deposited them in the cave. He quickly pulled them towards where he knew the bolt was, even before his eyes had adjusted. But just a moment after entering the cave his Zodiac hit something solid and lurched to a stop. Martina was thrown down in the front of the boat.

"Hey!" echoed from the cave. And then a loud splash.

"What the?" Kane managed.

And before he knew it, there was Fabrizzio grabbing the painter on the bow and hauling himself into the Zodiac beside Martina.

"What are you doing here?" Martina asked.

"It is so nice to see you too," Fabrizzio answered. He did not even acknowledge Kane's presence.

"What are you doing on my problem?" she asked.

"Your problem? Did you buy this cave? This rock?"

"You know what I mean. Why are you here? Are you trying to steal from me again? Can you never stop?"

"Me steal from you? After everything you have done to me?"

"Me? Done to you? How dare you?"

Fabrizzio stood. Shook the water from his long hair.

"Dare? I do what I want. You should know that."

Kane finally gathered his wits and tied off the Zodiac.

"Martina. Are you alright?" he asked.

"Doctore Kane," Fabrizzio hissed. "You untie this boat, and you go back. She stay with me."

"Are you insane? She's not staying with you."

"Really? I think she does. I think she stays. We ask her. Martina. Do you stay with me? Here? In the cave?"

"No. You go. You leave my cave."

"But don't you think of it as *our* cave? Since we so recently made love here? Since we found the problem? And the writing?"

Kane could not believe what he was hearing. Fabrizzio was saying that he and Martina had found the problem, and the writing. And that they had made love in the cave! He simply could not believe it. He looked to Martina for some sign, some argument. But there was none to be had.

"So it's true?" he asked.

Martina hung her head.

"I told you fat old puppy Kane. You go. She stays with me."

"No Fabrizzio. I no stay with you. I never stay with you ever again.

"Oh? And what if I go? If I tell everyone what I know? Is that what you want?"

Martina said nothing.

"You wouldn't. It would ruin you too."

"What are you talking about?" Kane said.

"So he doesn't know? You never told him?"

"Told me what?" Kane asked.

"Tell him," Fabrizzio said. "Tell him and see if he will still be your little lost puppy dog. See if he will still follow you around like a lost old man. Tell him."

"You tell him," Martina said.

"Yes. I tell him."

Fabrizzio jumped from Kane's Zodiac to his own. He reached into his water proof bag and when his hand emerged, the knife from the woman's home flashed in the reflected sun.

"Yes. I tell him. I tell him everything. I tell him that I cut your leg so you no dance no more. I tell him I cut you because you love Mikhail not me. I tell him I kill Marcello, because you want me to. I tell him everything."

"You are crazy," Kane said. "None of that is true. She cut her leg when she fell in her flat in Moscow. And Marcello, and the girls, that was kidnappers."

"No. No kidnappers. Just bad men that I pay."

"Impossible. It's not true. Tell him he's crazy Martina," Kane said.

Martina said nothing. Her head hung. Tears dripped from her eyes.

"You see. She does not correct me. Is true," Fabrizzio said.

Kane could not believe it. Would not believe it. He moved towards Martina in the front of the boat. He sat beside her, took her hand. Lifted her eyes to his.

"It can't possibly be true."

"He cut me. He cut my leg so I no dance."

"Why isn't he in jail? How can you even look at him? How can you even be anywhere near him?"

"Because I loved him."

"Love? It is impossible to love someone who severs your Achilles tendon. Impossible. It is impossible to love someone who kills your husband, and children. Impossible. It can't be."

"No Kane. It is not impossible. You ask the heroin man in the street and he will tell you he loves his heroin. And the woman, in the house, with the boy. She said she loved him."

"So you had him kill Marcello?"

"No. I had no idea. Until just now, I never knew."

"You knew," Fabrizzio said. "You wanted it."

"No. You are wrong. I loved Marcello."

"Loved him? But you were always with me. Always me.

You told me you wanted to be with me. So I arranged it. Like you wanted it. So you could be with me."

"No. You are wrong. You were wrong. How could you?"

"How could he? He's a lunatic. He's a killer. He cut your Achilles tendon so you couldn't dance. So you would be dependent on him. That's how he could. And look at him now. Is that the same knife? Is that how he crippled you? Ruined your career? Is that the knife?"

"Yes you old man. Yes it was this knife. I cut her. I cut her. Would you have used this knife? On Judith? Could you? Or were you a coward and just put something in her food, in her coffee? A coward and old man."

"It wasn't like that," Kane answered.

"I know. You a coward. Not like me. I take what I want. And I want her right now. So now I cut you. And feed you to the sea. And then I take her, and cut her, and feed her to the sea. And everyone think you do it to her, or you do it together. It no matter…"

Fabrizzio stepped to the edge of his Zodiac, then stepped across. He moved the two steps towards Kane and slashed once, then again with his knife. Kane retreated towards the little windscreen by the steering wheel. There was nowhere to go.

Fabrizzio swung again, then again. Laughing as he cut Kane's upraised arms. Laughing as Kane fell into the back of the Zodiac. Laughing as he raised the knife for the final fatal plunge…

Once

As Kane stood there transfixed in the moonlight, one day became the next. They were both leaving today. A day late, a day after the cave. After a day spent with the Caribineri and cameras and too many people. A bad day, a very bad day. Followed by last night, on the rooftop patio, with Martina.

A day when Mario had had to explain a dozen times how he had come across the scene in the cave he was going to study. A day when Mario had had to explain more than a dozen times how he had shot Fabrizzio dead just as Fabrizzio was about to kill Kane. A day when Kane's arms had been stitched over a hundred times. A day when Martina and Kane had been separated by the police, and then finally allowed to see each other for a few moments, during which they promised to keep their date on the rooftop, though a day late.

He knew this morning they would start the lengthy journeys that would take them back to their other lives. So he willed the moon to stop its flight across the warm Italian sky. As he did, he brought his hand slowly to his face, closed his eyes, and imagined her there. Her kisses still lay softly on his cheeks, on his neck, on his lips. If only he could stop the moon he could make this night and these kisses last forever. If only he could push the moon backwards once around the earth then Fabrizzio would be alive and he would not know that Martina had stayed with him even after what he had done.

Though he reached up and up, he could not reach the moon, and could not undo any of it.

And yet, he could still feel her long slender fingers as they rested in his, even after he'd realized what she'd known for some time. That although he would love her forever, that although she would always be a necessary part of him, and that although he would long for her every day, he knew that theirs were not lives to be spent together. He knew her life could and would and had to go on without him, and that he must find a way to go on without her. That they could likely never overcome the cave, or the tide, or the flood, or the interview, or any of it. That although he was powerless in her presence, her love was going to ruin him. And it had started. She had said herself that she was certain she would ruin him. Or more correctly, she would watch and let him ruin himself in her. Destroy himself, become something other, something less than what he was. Not Kane. He would do it knowingly, willingly, obsessively, and it would ruin him and anything they'd ever shared. Sadly, ironically, he realized it had also given him back his voice. Yes, it was ironic that he had found and lost his muse in such a short time. And that while she was gone, whatever power she had stirred in him remained. He was writing, dozens and dozens of pages at a time. Had almost completed his new novel, had written several poems, had started yet another novel.

He replayed for the hundredth time the night they had just shared.

"You know how much I like you, how much I love you," he'd said. He'd waited for her to stop him, but she hadn't.

"You know how I feel when we're together, when you're in my arms, when the entire world falls away and there's only you and me and us and now." Again he'd waited for her to stop him. But again she hadn't. She'd edged closer, held his hand more firmly, looked even more deeply into his eyes. Letting him go on, letting him get it out all at once, knowing it had to be done and said so she could end it. She knew the pain that would be wrought, and knew that it was unavoidable, necessary, inevitable, brutal, and yet compassionate.

"It's our last day. I've tried not to be sad, to not let tomorrow ruin today. But there's no other way to say this. I love you, I want you, I want to be with you, want to have all our tomorrows together. Even with everything, even with the cave, and Fabrizzio, and everything, I still want you."

Still she stayed silent. Held him with her eyes. Let him, made him go on.

"I'll love you forever and hold you every morning and every night and love you until the end of time."

He stopped. He took a deep breath, and let it out. He stared.

She put her hand on his shoulder, raised up on tip toes, and kissed him, lightly at first, then with a passion that matched his confession. She kissed his lips, his cheek, his neck, and then she stepped back.

"No," she said. "We can't have it. Any of it. There can't even be one tomorrow. There can only be tonight. And then nothing more. You know it."

Now he stood silent, waiting, his heart breaking. His tomorrows snatched away, made even worse by her kisses.

"No-one will ever love me more," she said. "I know that. No-one will ever care for me the way you do. I know that too. But it can't be. We can't work. Here, for a few days we were happy. But even that happiness cost too much. The tide. The flood. The fall. Then Fabrizzio, and the cave. It has cost too much. Those are things we can never forget, never undo."

"Even though you made me see him for what he was. Only having you right beside him let me see him for the first time. I thank you for that. I'll always thank you for that. For the laughter, for the moonlight, for the climbing, for you, for everything. In some way you've made me whole again. After so so long." She paused, looked away into the night.

"Then why? Why can't it work?" he asked. "Even when we have promised ourselves next year?"

She turned back to him.

"Kane. Be real. Who could ever forget it all? The tide, the flood, the fall, the cave? You know it," she said. "You know." Her voice was soft but her words were hard, sharp, precise, relentless, correct. "It's right there to see. Just open your eyes for one minute and you'll see it."

Now he turned away and stared out over the silvery moonlit washed Mediterranean. He tried to see it, and slowly, then suddenly, all at once knew she was right. And at the exact moment when he knew he would never be the same and would always feel the active ache of her loss, at the exact moment when he knew they would never be together, at that moment he felt her arms surround him, engulf him, consume him, draw him in like he had never been drawn before. He felt her kisses on his neck, felt her lips brush against his ear, and heard her whisper.

Upon accepting that he could not have her forever, that he could only have her on her terms, in her way, this one time, she gave herself to him, for just this now.

"Take me now, love me now, give me this one last thing, then let me go. Here and now, just this once. Let me know you can know me and let me be. In this tiny moment of perfection, a perfect place and perfect time and perfect love that rises above everything else. This one little moment of perfect. Now, Kane. Let me have the best of you, of me, of here. Let it bathe us, wash over us, become a part of us and of always and of all our tomorrows. Let it wash it all away. Let this be the one thing we remember about Sardinia. So everything else will go away."

She slipped out of her loose black dress, took his hand, closed her eyes, and brought her lips to his.

Departure

Katia waited with the engine running. Her little leased car idled in front of Martina's boutique hotel. Mina's bags were already in the back seat, and in the trunk, and Mina was giving one last good-bye kiss to the old men who had cared for her the past month, and in years gone by. Finally she left them and joined Katia in the car.

"Your flight is in two hours, and it takes an hour to get to the airport," Katia said.

"So we have time for one little errand," Martina said.

"It's your funeral," Katia said.

"Prego, we go down the hill, to Kane's hotel."

"I thought you already said good-bye, last night."

"Si. We say good-bye. I no see him. But I give him this," she said. Martina held up a small envelope.

"What is it?" Katia asked.

"A map. To the cave, to the climbs, and to the clinic."

"I think he knows where they are," Katia said.

"Si. But he needs to know that I know too."

Kane placed his bag by the front door of his hotel. Tetsiana looked up from behind the counter, then stood and came around to embrace him.

"We miss you Doctore Kane," she said.

"I will be back next year," he said.

"Si?" she asked. "Still?"

"Si. Still."

"You finish your story?" she asked.

"Si. It is finished. And the next one started."

"Will you send me a copy? With your autograph?" she asked.

"Si. I will mail it. Or I can give it to you in person next year."

"Oh. Please mail it. I want to read it and then ask you all about it when you stay with us next year. You stay with us next year no?"

"Si. Next year. I stay with you. In the same room, on the same days, and some extra days as well. And I eat breakfast in the sunny room, and eat my dinners under the moon and oleanders. And I drink wine on the rooftop and think and write and climb and run."

"You no miss her too much? It no hurt too much?"

"Part of me believes that she will be here too," he said. "Part of me will always believe that. And even if she isn't actually here, you know that she will be here," he held his hands over his heart. He took the envelope from his jacket pocket, unfolded the little map, traced his hand over the pictures of the cave and the clinic and the rooftop terrace where she had given herself to him just last night, just twelve hours before. He carefully refolded the map, placed it back in his pocket, and headed for the door.

Running
Sudbury, Ontario
Two months later

Kane sat stiffly, the collar of his tuxedo chafing at his neck. The speakers at the medical conference in the small mining city in Ontario droned on and on and on. Only two months removed from Sardinia, Kane was almost all the way back into his earlier life. His life "before Mina," or simply "before."

Kane sat with his colleague's wife.

"You'll never guess who I saw last week?" the wife asked.

"Who?" Kane asked. Perhaps this piece of trivia would add an ounce of interest to an otherwise interminable dinner at the medical conference his hospital forced him to attend annually. Since his only friend at the conference was speaking, and thus sitting at the head table, Kane was seated here alone but for his friend's wife and some others he did not know.

"That dancer you know. What's her name?"

"Dancer?"

"Yes. You know. The one the magazines said you were dating?"

"Martina?"

"Yes. That's it. Martina Fucentese."

Though months had gone by, it was all suddenly right there again. Kane felt the incompleteness again, and the jealousy. And the longing. Felt that it had to be wrong that anyone else would see her, talk to her, be near her, enjoy her, and he not be a part of it. He fought it. She wasn't his. She'd made that clear. Still, he felt it, so he fought it. Tried to remember his promise. To add, not to subtract, not to take, to add to both their lives, to add to her as she'd let him.

"And you'll never guess who I saw her with."

Agony.

"Who?" Kane asked. Inviting it now. Peeling the covering off the wound, exposing the raw part, waiting for the searing pain, the acid burn, in the freshly exposed wound.

"Baryshnikov".

"Mikhail Baryshnikov?"

"Yes."

Of course Kane knew they'd been together. A couple. All

those years ago at the Bolshoi. Before his escape to New York, before her escape to Buenos Aries. When Russia had been behind the Iron Curtain. They had been each other's escape. A fairy tale romance between the maestro and the diva. Rex and Regina.

"They were dancing!"

"Dancing?" Kane asked. He knew this was impossible. But humored his colleague's wife.

"Yes."

"Dancing how?"

"Ballet dancing."

Kane fixed her with a stare. Doubted her words. He'd read the stories, heard her tale of the injury, and Fabrizzio's revelation. He had seen the scar. Had seen the knife that Fabrizzio had wielded to make that scar. And he had seen her movements. Though he'd seen her move on the rock and felt her move beneath him, above him, as part of him, with him inside her, he doubted this last detail. Doubted that she could dance. Or would even try.

"Oh?"

"Well, only sort of. They were teaching, and just showing a couple of positions."

"Teaching?"

"Yes. At the Bolshoi. Kind of a celebrity alumni thing."

"What were you doing there?" Kane asked.

"I was there with Paul. Our annual trip. You remember? You even went with us that one time."

Kane remembered it all. That's where they'd met. Or, at least that was when he'd seen her the first time. Back before she was Regina. Back when she was becoming. Of course he remembered. Hadn't he re-discovered the poems from back then? The sophomoric love-sick poetry filled with simple longing? Yes he remembered.

"Yes, I remember."

"Well there we were, and we saw an advert that Baryshnikov was going to be there at the clinic, so we went. Paul knows him, you know. So we went. It was great. He remembered Paul and so we got to talk to him, to them. He was what I thought. She wasn't."

Slowly he framed the question. Discarded it. Framed

another. Discarded that one as well. How could he ask? He couldn't. Couldn't. Could not reveal how much he felt, how much he hurt, how desperately he wished he'd been there, seen it, even if it meant seeing her with him. Could not reveal the pain, even to himself. The exquisiteness of the thought was too much. He pretended his pager had buzzed.

"I've got to go. Tell Paul I'm sorry I missed his speech. It was nice to see you," Kane said. He rose, turned, and walked away. Walked slowly at first, felt every eye in the banquet hall was on him. Felt every heart and every head saw his pain, laughed at him, judged him as being too weak, mocked him for even trying to live in the realm of the gods, of the great, when he was simply Kane.

He left the hall, and walked more quickly, towards the exit from the hotel. An exit. An escape. He pushed through the revolving doors into the night air. Felt the void inside him, pulling him forward, pulling at his center, pulling at who he was. He began to run. A block passed by. Faster, another block. Until his lungs cried and copper tasted in his mouth and block after block stretched out behind him, separating him from the dinner, and the Bolshoi, and Baryshnikov, and Martina. City center turned to city edge, and yet he ran as fast as he could. Until the edges of his vision blurred and until the screaming ache in his lungs and legs masked the other hurt, the one he feared would never heal. The one he feared just might.

Kane sat alone in his hotel room. His fingers touched the keyboard. He entered his search. Bolshoi Baryshnikov Fucentese benefit 2008. And there it was. It was true. All of it. With pictures, and quotes, and "what does it all mean" analysis. Minutes turned to hours as the obsession took hold. And then the words spoke to him, directly to him. Telling him that they would be doing another benefit together in six months, at the end of the current school session for the incoming dancers. In six months, just four months before their fairy tale date in Sardinia, with the cave, the clinic, and the children.

On the desk beside the computer lay a pen and a small pad of hotel paper. Kane touched the pen, rolled it in his fingers. Put it down, put his fingers back on the keyboard, then took the pen

back in his hand. He clicked it open, touched pen to paper, and wrote:
 Mina's eyes
 Where waves meet sky
 Blue on blue
 Liquid jewels
 Infinity tried....

Russia
Six months later

Kane was washing his hands after a half a day volunteering at the small clinic in the poor Russian suburb. His mentor and friend was washing his hands beside him.

"Are you sure you can go back there? After everything?"

"I'm sure I have to try. And I'm sure the children need me. I said I would do it, but more than that, I want to do it, for the children."

"Only for the children? Aren't you secretly hoping she'll be there?"

"No. There is no secret hope. I know she will be there. I know exactly when, and I know exactly where. If there was only secret hope, then I'd go see her tonight. And try to convince her to honor the promise she made last year."

"Tonight? What do you mean go see her tonight?"

"Yes tonight. She's here. Didn't you know? Doing a benefit with Baryshnikov."

"Here?"

"Yes."

"Is that why you had to do a reading here in Russia? Tonight? Because of the benefit?"

Kane said nothing.

"Kane I've known you these twenty years. And I've never seen you do something like this. You wouldn't even scheme something like this in your novels."

"This isn't a novel."

Martina sat outside in the northern Russian late summer evening. She sat across from her one time lover, Mikhail Baryshnikov. Small cups of thick Turkish coffee sitting on the table between them steamed in the cool evening air.

"I am happy you are here, but I still don't understand," he said.

"Yes you do. Is for the children," she said.

"Ah yes, the children," he answered.

"Then why are you leaving? Going back to the island?"

"Also for the children. At the clinic."

"The clinic? With the doctor?"

Martina said nothing.

"After everything? After Fabrizzio?"

She sipped from her coffee, looked into the sky, then looked back to him.

"I expected him to call. Or to write. Or to seek me out and find me and talk to me. But he never did."

"Who?"

"The doctor, the writer."

"Ah yes, the writer," he said.

"He sent me a birthday present. It was an odd present. It was a picture of himself as a child. In the card he said it was from when he was innocent. And that he longed to create, or at least preserve, that innocence for others."

"Yes. You are right. It was odd."

Kane walked slowly down the twilit sidewalk. Lovers walked hand in hand in the late summer evening, not quite a white night, but still one of those lengthy twilights that seem to make everything move more slowly, and seem somehow softer around the edges.

"Kane? Is that you?" Martina asked.

Kane stopped, turned towards her voice.

"Yes. Is that you?" he asked in turn.

"Yes. What are you doing here? We were just talking about you!"

"Oh?"

"Yes. Kane, this is my friend Mikhail. Mikhail this is Doctore Kane, the writer."

Mikhail stood, bent his head in a polite yet aristocratic bow, and then extended his hand. After shaking Kane's hand he swept his hand in a graceful invitation towards the table. His eyes were inviting, genuine, instantly putting Kane at ease, instantly making Kane like him.

"Join us, please," he asked.

"No, I'm sorry, I am late. I did not expect to see you here," Kane said.

"Nor I you," she answered.

Kane's mind went blank. Of course he knew she was here, in this city, in this time. And he was certain that she had no idea that he was here. His reading had been advertised, but he knew she never read the papers, or watched television. There was her immediate world, her next climb, her next meal, and there was nothing else. There was no way she would have known. He had scheduled this trip so he could see her on the stage, see her with the children, not so she could see him.

"What are you late for?" she asked.

"For the theatre, down the street. I am doing a reading tomorrow, and we need to rehearse, the lights, the microphones."

"A reading?" she asked.

"Yes. And I am late. They have already called me twice. Will you be here for long? Can I come back and have a coffee with you? This will only take an hour."

"No. I am sorry. We have to go to the theatre. We were just going to leave."

"To the theatre?"

"Yes. We are dancing a benefit tomorrow."

"You are dancing?" he asked.

"Just a little. Mostly I stand and gesture." Martina moved her arms from position to position.

"When is it?" he said.

"Tomorrow. At two. Can you come?" she asked.

"Yes. But just for a little. My reading is at five. Will you come to the reading? After you are done?"

"I'll try," she said.

Kane's phone rang. He looked at the display, pressed the silence button, and put it back in his pocket.

"I didn't think it would be like this," she said.

"What?" he asked.

"I knew I would see you again. Sometime, somewhere, probably on the island. I knew. But I didn't think it would be like this. I always thought, somehow, that there would be moonlight, and the sea."

Her eyes temporarily drifted off and focused on the mental image she had created.

"Tomorrow, please come to the reading."

"I will try," she said.

She rose, kissed the air beside both of his cheeks, then kissed him gently on the lips. "I will try," she said.

Kane turned, and hurried down the street, leaving Martina

and Mikhail alone at the table.

"Tomorrow he reads from his book of poems," he said.

"Book of poems?" she asked.

"Yes. It's lovely. I have read it twice, some of the poems I have read many times. I never cared for his novels. And then there was that ugliness with his wife. But these poems. These poems I like. They are sad, yet humorous, very Russian. There's two about a dancer. Any idea who that might be? One that is very funny. One that is tres romantique. From the look of love in his eyes I suspect you are the dancer. And from the look of fear in your eyes, I suspect you will go to his reading. But I don't know whether you will like the poems. Perhaps you should go to him, at least to the reading. Ease his pain."

"I've heard one of the poems already," she said.

Mikhail said nothing. Sipped from his espresso. Prodded her with his eyes.

"The funny poem. Only it wasn't very funny when I heard it.

Benefit

Kane looked around the dance theatre. It was much as he remembered it from his other visit here, when he had seen Martina dance all those years before. She was there, with Baryshnikov, that was also the same. They stood together near the stage, smiling, fielding questions. His hand was gently about her waist. Not a possessive grasp, not like Fabrizzio, but still about her waist.

Kane stopped to lift a glass of wine from a silver platter. He sipped, watched, took another step towards the couple.

"Doctor Kane?" he heard.

He turned towards the voice.

"You are the last person I expected to see here," the reporter said.

"And you I," he returned. "What are you doing here?" he asked.

"Observing. Listening. Watching. Letting it unfold in front of me," she answered.

"So you were listening back on the island?" Kane said.

"Si," she answered.

Kane could feel the questions building in her. Could feel the story lines taking directions, progressing in those directions. He waited for what would surely be the first of many impatient questions. None came.

He sipped from his wine, she sipped from hers.

Kane looked around the room, saw several of the children in their costumes, children who would soon dance the benefit with Martina and Kane on the stage. Finally he returned his eyes towards the stage. Martina was smiling her "public Mina" smile, and though Mikhail's hand was on her waist, she was maintaining a gap between her and him.

"Describe how she looks," Kane said to the reporter.

"You," she replied.

"Well done," Kane answered. "She looks like a woman who is doing a duty. This meet and greet must be hard for her, because she is about to dance. For her it is about the dance, from the stage. Lifting us through her performance. It is not about this. Talking, laughing, touching people. Though she undoubtedly touches us all, she prefers to do it from a distance, from the stage, above us."

"Oh?" the reporter prodded.

"Very well done," Kane said. "Now you have the hang of it. But even though she will only touch us from up there, that is only because there are so many of us. If there was only one, or a small group of friends, she would be different. The smile would be different, there would be no space between her and the person with their arm about her. She can give herself, almost completely, but not like this."

"Um hmm," the reporter prodded.

"I came to watch her dance. But I can't stay for the whole performance, can only stay for a few moments. I am doing a reading, just down the street. I am reading some poems. You've already heard the funny poem."

"Poems?" she said.

"Yes poems. From my new work. The new novel comes out soon, and I will read the first pages, and some pages from the middle. Then I will read three poems. If you are done here, why don't you come? Don't get the wrong idea. I invited Martina, in fact, off the record, I arranged the whole thing so we would overlap. So I'd get the chance to see her. And then quite unexpectedly she saw me too. So I invited her. She said she would try. Maybe you could help get her there?"

"Yes. I will try. But aren't you supposed to work together in the clinic in a few weeks? Won't you see her then?"

"Yes. But I wanted to try to recast the spell before we arrived. It's been almost a year. And this is the first time I've seen her. In fact, in this whole year I only sent her one card, a birthday card. No calls, no letters, no emails. And nothing from her. I know we will be back on the island, and I was hoping to correct a mistake I made before we got back there, so it wouldn't be odd at the start, or awkward. So that we'd both know what it was going to be before we got there."

The reporter extended her hand. "Good luck," she said.

Kane shook her hand, then stepped away from her and towards the small group surrounding Martina and Kane.

"Doctor Kane," Mikhail greeted him. He released his hand from Martina's waist and extended it to shake. They shook, and then Mikhail took a graceful quarter step back to allow Kane closer to Martina. He expected her to kiss the air beside his cheeks but she made no step towards him. Instead, she extended her hand to shake. Kane took her hand, but instead of shaking, he bent in a shallow bow, and gently kissed the back of her hand.

"Bellisima," he whispered as he returned her hand from his embrace.

"Kane. I so glad you make it," she said.

The small group looked from Martina to Kane, then back. Some recognized him, some did not.

"Yes. I would not have missed it."

"You are reading tonight no?"

"Yes. So I can only stay for a little while, just the first pas de deux."

Martina's eyes refocused out of Kane's sphere and into the wider sphere of the small group around them.

"Kane is a writer. I am certain many of you know his work. Tonight he is reading from his new novel, and from a new book of poetry. After we dance, if there is time, I go down the street to hear the end of his reading."

Kane felt his heart first skip a beat and then hammer hard against his ribs. He first lost his breath, and then sucked in a saving lungful.

"Good luck," Mikhail said to Kane. "Now we dance!"

He took Martina's hand, guided her away from the group, away from Kane, and up to the stage. The first strains of the opening dance signaled the patrons to take their seats. Kane retreated to the back of the theatre, rejoining the reporter.

She said nothing, simply guiding Kane to the seat beside her.

"Could be quite a story to tell after tonight," Kane said. "Especially if both she and you make it to my reading."

The lights went down in the theatre, and the ballet began.

Reading

Kane accepted the applause from his readers, his listeners. He had completed the second of his two poems, and still had not seen Martina enter the theatre. He had alerted the theatre owners that Martina might be arriving late. He had given them instructions about showing her to the front of the theatre, to seats he had reserved. One for Martina, and one for Mikhail, and another for the reporter, just in case.

The master of ceremonies and host signaled that Kane would take another two questions from the audience before beginning his last poem for the evening.

A beautiful young man rose to his feet, glided to the microphone in the aisle, and smiled at Kane.

"Maestro. Your words this evening are so lovely. They are much different from your earlier work, which, we all know, can be ruthless at times. So, may I ask what brought about this change? Was it the dancer? Is she your inspiration? Your mistress?"

Kane focused on the young man. Sipped from the crystal goblet of water in his left hand. Considered not answering, then considered answering. As he considered, he scanned the crowd one more time, his eyes coming to rest on the empty seats in the front row.

Interpreting the pause as an insult, the master of ceremonies spoke to the question. "Sir you go too far," the master of ceremonies answered. "Next question."

At that moment, Kane saw a movement at the back of the theatre. It was Martina, she had arrived. Alone. No Mikhail, just Martina. She was still dressed in her costume from the dance.

A ripple formed in the audience as they recognized her. The ripple grew in intensity as she moved slowly, but intently, towards the stage. Soon every eye in the theatre was on her as she arrived in front of the stage. Kane moved towards her, but she held up her hand, found her seat, turned and waved to the audience, then sat. She motioned Kane to continue.

Kane raised the microphone.

"Sir, the answers to your questions are, in order, love, yes, yes, and none of your business. You should know better than to ask such a question. Now, for the final reading of this evening."

Kane signaled to the master of ceremonies.

The man nodded to Kane, regained his polite master of ceremony voice, and introduced the Legend of Mina's leg.

Martina's eyes first registered shock, then disappointment. She rose to her feet, waved again to the crowd, and stepped towards the aisle.

Kane jumped to his feet.

"Wait," he called out.

Martina stopped, turned, a tear already forming in her eye. Her only thought was how could she have been so foolish? How could she let him embarrass her again, in public, here, after everything?

"Wait," he said more gently.

Kane signaled to the master of ceremonies to leave the stage, to take a seat down below.

"There has been change in the schedule," Kane said.

"Tonight, I get the rarest chance a man can ever have. I get a chance to make right something that I did wrong. So, please indulge me while I read this poem, that has never been read before, and that will only be read tonight. Originally this poem was just for me, was just a passion I embraced. But tonight, I hope it can be my redemption. I had hoped to read it in private, but I suspect I will never get another chance after tonight if I do not read it now. So, I read it here, and pray for my one chance at overcoming my earlier mistake."

Martina took a step back towards her seat.

"Please," he said to her. He motioned to the steps at the edge of the stage.

Martina took a tentative step towards the steps, questioning him with her posture, with her pace, with her eyes.

"Please," he said again. He walked towards the steps, extended his hand to help her up, and took her hand as she alit upon the steps.

He walked with her towards his chair, sat her down, kissed her gently on the cheek, and took two steps away.

Kane pulled folded sheets from his shirt pocket.

He straightened them, surveyed the audience, cleared his throat, bent to one knee before her, and began to read, his eyes never leaving hers. His voice was unlike anything she had heard from him. In it, she felt the emotion, and the love, she knew he felt for her. In it, she felt the loss that she dared not to admit.

Mina's eyes
Waves meet sky
Blue on blue
Liquid jewels
Truth inside

Instantly she was back in Italy, back on the island, back on the rock. He continued.

Mina's touch
Waves above
Limestone soft
On the rock
On my neck

Mina's eyes
Sea meets sky
Gaze holds touch
Single kiss
Night air moon

Mina's touch
Sky to sand
Warmth at night
Touch holds hands
Touch and stand

Mina's eyes
Night meets wine
Azure depths
No fine line
Stand and hold

Mina's touch
Beach below
Smile on sand
Hold touch voids
Voids hold touch

Mina's eyes
See meets why
Blue are mine
On her eyes
In her touch

Mina's touch
Waves and breeze
On my eyes
In my touch

Mina's eyes
Touch the Sea.
Close your eyes,
open your mind,
open your eyes
open me.

Mina's eyes.
Mina's eyes.

Martina stood slowly from the chair, crossed the short but infinite space between them, and took him in her arms. He kissed her. She kissed him back. For a moment, for a second, for an eternity that opened before them. She stepped out of his arms, kissed him lightly, then broke free of his embrace.

"Thank you," she said.

She kissed him again, stepped away, and left the stage. A very dramatic exit.

Kane watched her as she went, knowing he had done everything he could to put things right, to say what he wanted to say, to say what he needed to say. He yearned to leap down from the stage, to run after her, to beg her to stay with him. Yet he knew that was the most certain way to drive her so far away he would never see her again.

The audience watched her leave, watched him rooted to the stage, and remained silent, shocked at the raw display of love and emotion. Seeing all, comprehending none.

Chalk
Two Months Later

Early autumn sunlight angled down through the dusty window on the clinic set high in the hills above Dorgali. The air was scented with the end of summer, and the coming of fall. Kane looked up from the next to last patient, his gaze drifting out the window, and onto the mountains framed therein. He drew a deep deliberate breath and released it slowly. Kane rolled his head slowly in circles, left to right, then right to left. He walked towards the window and looked to the left. The large boulder sat unmoved.

How long it had been since he stood atop it with Martina? What a series of events that first ascent had wrought. The walk into the interior, the confrontation with Fabrizzio, the substitution of the funny poem for the love poem at the dinner, the separation, the killing, the longing. Kane closed his eyes, drew in another deep deliberate breath, and once again released it.

He visualized the tension in his back leaving his body with each breath. He visualized the movements that would take him around the boulder, his new project, the traversal, that he had been working for nearly a month, alone. Trying to complete the circle, to return from where he had begun, around and around he had gone, never completing the project, never completing the journey. Feeling that just one more move would get him through the crux and let him complete the circle.

His mind drifted, as it so often did, to Martina. He knew she could figure it out for him. But she had not returned to the clinic with him. She was here, and they had seen each other. But it had been stiff, nearly formal. Not what he'd expected after their moment in Moscow. His position was clear. He loved her, and he wanted her, but he would not take, would not demand, and would not settle for anything less than her love in return. So he waited, with hope. Hope that she would accept his love, accept him, and join him, once and for always. Not just once, like on the rooftop on that magical and cursed night last year. Not just on her terms. But for always.

Kane took and released another breath. He returned to the clinic. His mind shifting from the boulder and all it represented to the last patient. It was the boy, with his mother. The boy who had been treated so often for the cuts and bruises and fractures. Today there were no cuts, no downturned faces, no hidden shame. Today the boy simply had a fever, which Kane quickly traced to an infected scrape on his shin. Kane cleaned the scrape, dressed it, and gave the boy a shot of Penicillin. He handed a bottle of liquid to the woman, and explained that the boy should drink a capful twice a day.

The mother thanked Kane. Her eyes held none of the fear or the anger from the last time he had seen her, when she had slapped Martina for driving Fabrizzio from her home. She had come to accept her life without Fabrizzio, without the constant pain. Her eyes told Kane all of this as she smiled, collected her boy, and set off down the path that would lead to the interior.

Kane washed his hands.

He sat on the bench near the door. He reached up and removed his climbing shoes and chalk bag from the peg beside the door. He removed his doctor shoes, removed his socks, and kneaded his toes. He rolled his ankles, stretched his fingers, and once again rolled his head in circles. When he was done, he pulled on his sandals, stood, and walked out of the clinic, taking the few steps to the boulder. The chalk bag was in his right hand.

Kane looked back over his shoulder to savor the valley, the clay tiled roof on the clinic, and the mountains beyond. Its beauty washed over him, and for one moment he was at peace. Tranquility. Where had it gone? Had it vanished forever at that dinner, in that cave? Or did it simply lay dormant, waiting, for a time like this, for a place like this, and for the woman he loved. Could she ever love him again?

He lay down in the grass near the boulder, placing the chalk bag beside him. He rolled his knees to one side, stretching his back, and then to the other. As he stretched he heard a car working its way slowly up the steep rutted path towards the clinic. He was expecting no-one, and the last patient had been seen.

Kane returned to his stretching, pulling his knees towards his chest, trying to remember all the stretches, the entire routine that Martina had taught him. The car drew closer, Kane could hear it accelerate slowly out of each of the hairpin turns that ended the drive to the clinic.

Kane stood, approached the boulder, and began to stretch his fingers against the rock. He loved this first touch of the rock. Each time it was a portal from the horizontal world to the vertical. From a world where everything was flat, to a world with edges, and knobs, and ripples, and features. From a world upon which people walked, to a world in which people climbed. From a world that spanned from ground to sky and horizon to horizon to a smaller more intense world that spanned the breadth of your reach and the breadth of your steps. From there, to here.

The car made the last turn, drove the last yards to the cleared patch of dirt and rock in front of the clinic, and stopped.

Kane placed his right hand on a hold on the rock, held it, and turned his body towards the car. He felt the stretch in his elbow, his shoulder, his back.

Martina stepped from the car.

Kane held his stretch. As it had in Russia, his heart first stopped, then began to hammer incessantly in his chest. His lungs shrank to the size of raisins and he found it hard to catch his breath.

She closed the car door, walked around behind the car, and opened the hatch back. She reached in and emerged with two pairs of climbing shoes.

Kane raised an eyebrow. He let go of the rock with his right hand, grasped it with his left. He turned his body, now stretching his left elbow, his left shoulder, his back. His eyes never left her, his touch never left the rock.

She closed the hatch back, then walked towards him. He knew that walk. He loved that walk. Her pace, measured, confident, slightly uneven, indelibly etched in his mind. He knew he could live his whole life just watching her walk.

Kane released the rock. He bent into the grass, retrieved his chalk bag.

Martina smiled at him, but said nothing.

She looked at the rock, saw the chalk marks leading around the boulder. She moved slowly, following the chalk marks, around the boulder to the right, then re-appearing from the left.

She looked one more time at the rock, then at Kane.

She sat. She took the first pair of shoes and placed them beside her. She placed the second pair between them, offering them as a gift.

He took a step towards her, picked them up, looked at his old, battered pair, and sat.

He removed his old shoes, replacing them with hers.

Still not a word was spoken.

She stood, touched the rock, then stepped back.

She motioned towards the rock, inviting Kane to go first.

Once again he picked up the chalk bag from where he had placed it in the grass. He swung it behind him, drew the ends of the cord together, and tied a small knot at his waist. He put his right hand on the rock, then his left.

Martina slowly, ever so slowly, walked towards him, touched him on the shoulder, turned him towards her. He released the rock.

She kissed the air beside his right cheek, and then beside his left.

Her hands found the knot on the chalk bag, and gently untied it. She removed it from his waist, then fixed him for a moment with her eyes.

She looked into the chalk bag, considered all that was held inside. Not just the white powder to dry her hands, and his, but also the touches and the meaning and the history.

She swung the chalk bag behind her, drew the two strands of the cord in front of her, and firmly tied a knot about her waist.

Looking up from the knot, she found Kane's eyes.

Once again she kissed the air beside his right cheek, then beside his left.

"Chalk?" she asked.

The End

Read What Others Are Saying About JT's 1 Best-Selling TechnoThriller "The Pattern"

So, I am going to think twice before I get into that plane next time.

This story made me think about our trust and dependence that we so easily give up to the programmers of our daily life. Bravo Mister Kalnay for writing a thought provoking and entertaining look at the way our airliners operate today. The story was fast moving and gripping. I found myself laughing out loud from the witty banter between the characters.

Mister Kalnay gives us a look into the world of computer programming that touches so much our daily life that is enlightening and scary at the same time. He breathes life into the nameless people we rely on to protect us from all that could go wrong with the system. Could not put this one down...but I advise reading this one before you head to the airport anytime soon.

Yeah, it's gripping! Grips you and if, like me, you have to fly right afterwards, you'll be gripping the armrests the whole flight! Nice mix of interesting relationships, tech-savvy software lore, and mystery. Couldn't put it down!

The first of JT Kalnay's works I've read, this early effort compares nicely with Ryan's "Adolescence of P-1" or Grisham's "The Firm" but wisely navigates around Powers' "Galatea 2.2" territory. You get a good sense this writer has "been there" but there is more to "The Pattern" than just an insider's view of an industry and culture that is pretty much a black box to those that haven't. This one gets a 4 out of 5 simply for not quite cracking the level of the big boys: Clancy, Ludlum, Cussler et al. Will be interested to see how this author develops in this genre.

I was surprised to enjoy this book so much as it comes from a not so well known author. Fantastic fiction.

I was thinking about the HAL 9000 malfunction in 2001 A Space Odyssey while reading The Pattern. Decades ago, I wondered if people would risk their lives on software. Now we have fly-by-wire controls in our airplanes and we depend on software in our hospital equipment as well as our cars. Software glitches can now kill. It's a really scary thought and I really enjoyed the thrilling journey the author takes us on in this techno-thriller treat. In the best spirit of science fiction it gives us pause to consider the dependency we freely give to our technology. In addition, as this story unfolds our humanity is laid bare in the face of technological realities that are seldom realized by most of us.

Please enjoy this sample of The Pattern

June 19, 1994
Chantilly Virginia

Assembled From News Wire Reports

A chartered executive Lear Jet inbound from Mexico City crashed today in heavy fog during final approach to Dulles National Airport in Washington D.C. Ten passengers and two crew members were killed instantly. There were no Americans on the flight and there were no survivors. Although the airplane had the latest electronics, it had aborted one landing due to the fog and was in the process of lining up for a second attempt when the accident occurred. The black box flight recorder has been recovered from the wreckage and the bodies have been identified. The last transmission from the cockpit was, "There seems to be something wrong with the electronics. Going around." The plane disappeared from radar less than ten seconds later.

June 20, 1994
San Francisco, California

Thin clouds drifted high above the city by the Bay. Craig and Stacey sat behind the APSoft building on the large cedar deck. A gentle breeze caressed Stacey's long, summer golden hair. Craig was having a very hard time concentrating on the report in his hands.

"Do you want to hear something weird?" Stacey asked.

"I don't know. Do I?" Craig answered.

"Yes. You do," Stacey said.

"Okay. Let's have it," Craig said.

"We're three for three this year," Stacey said.

"I don't get it," Craig said.

"On airplane crashes. We're three for three."

"I still don't get it," Craig said.

"Listen. First you know that guy in Turkey where the Blackhawks got shot down. Second, we both know Rakesh who's been in Hong Kong where the plane that crashed in Nagoya originated. Third, my friend in Mexico works for that company that chartered that plane that crashed in Virginia the other day. We're three for three."

"Better call the National Enquirer," Craig said.

"Jerk," Stacey said.

"We know somebody at almost every airline or aircraft manufacturer in the world Stacey. It'd be a miracle if we didn't know someone somehow related to every crash," Craig said.

"You're still a jerk," Stacey said.

"Yeah I know. It's part of my charm," he replied.

Stacey made a face at him and rolled her eyes.

"Please," she said.

"But you know what? You've piqued my curiosity. I'm going to do some research and see how many wrecks there have been in the last year. It does seem like there's been an unusual amount doesn't it?" Craig asked.

"Nice try," Stacey said.

"No. I'm totally serious. Now that you've pointed it out, I really am curious."

"Um huh," she said dismissively.

"Ready to throw it some more," Stacey asked, dangling Craig's birthday Frisbee on the end of a long slender finger.

"Not right now," Craig said. I better get started on that research.

JT Kalnay is an attorney and an author. He has been an athlete, a soldier, a professor, a programmer, an Ironman, and mountain climber. JT now divides his time between being an attorney, being an author, and helping his wife chase after seven nieces and nephews.

JT was born and raised in Belleville, Ontario, Canada. Growing up literally steps from the Bay of Quinte, water, ice, fishing, swimming, boating, and drowning were very early influences and appear frequently in his work.

Educated at the Royal Military College, the University of Ottawa, the University of Dayton, and Case Western Reserve University, JT has spent countless hours studying a wide range of subjects including math, English, computer science, and law. Many of his stories are set on college campuses.

JT is a certified rock climbing guide and can often be found atop crags in West Virginia, California, Mexico, and Italy. Rock climbing appears frequently in his writing.

JT has witnessed firsthand many traumatic events including the World Trade Center Bombing, the Long Island Railroad Shooting, a bear attack, a plane crash, and numerous fatalities, in the mountains and elsewhere.

Connect with jt online at:
www.jtkalnay.com
http://jtkalnaynovels.wordpress.com

Made in the USA
Middletown, DE
14 November 2025